He, Him His

LK WOLLETT

Published by LK WOLLETT, 2023.

This is a work of fiction. Similarities to real people, places, or events are entirely coincidental.

HE, HIM HIS

First edition. August 29, 2023.

Copyright © 2023 LK WOLLETT.

ISBN: 979-8223041399

Written by LK WOLLETT.

He, Him, His

By LK Wollett

Book 1 - Chapter 1

1835 AD. Sometimes, as I stand at the kitchen sink, I can spot Jesse making his way around the curve, with his head down to overcome the gravity that wants to pull him back down the hill. If gravity could win, he would tumble three or so miles back to the wharf where his ship had come in hours before. Other times, his footsteps on the back porch alert me of his arrival. Either way, I'm usually not on his radar when he walks into the house. As soon as he takes off his back pack and boots, he lands in the old over-stuffed chair, lays his head back and rests. When we first moved in together, I tried to fuss over him, and he let me know with some irritation that it wasn't necessary. Because he won't share how he feels or what is happening to him, I have to guess he has expended himself on the ship and has to recharge.

His behavior, after landing in the chair, is quite inconsistent which I find rather exciting because I know, at some point, I will appear on his radar and he will ravage me like he was starving and I was his meal. I love the ravages because he gets personal and says my name, Beth. Sometimes, he pulls me into the chair and ravages me immediately. Most of the time, however, I'm given no clue if the ravaging will take place after a few hours sleep, after a meal, during a meal or during a bath, just to name a few possibilities. And, the entire length of his furlough, I can expect a ravaging at any time, any place - any place respectable, that is.

Because his arrival can be any day and any time of the day, I can't have anything planned for him so I have to have everything planned for him, if that makes sense. I assume every day he will arrive and on that day, I serve something he likes whether he is there or not. Every day, the house is clean for him. Every day, I wear something he likes and I look forward to him removing it.

Once he is recharged, bathed, fed and ravage-satisfied, he walks the few acres of his homestead, looking for repairs needed on the house or buildings. He always asks if everything in the house is working properly and I'll show him anything that needs attention. He also checks supplies and makes sure there is enough flour, salt and whatever else is required. He does nothing to make his life more complicated than this.

A few years ago, I was married, happily married, with three children. My house was further up the hill and my husband, Richard, worked in a government records office down by the wharf. We often passed Jesse's house which Richard and I thought was a mysterious place because the house was dark for weeks in a row then, without warning, a light would appear. At that time, we didn't know that Jesse was at sea. Richard finally met Jesse when some new regulation was passed and Jesse had to provide information to the government records office. I was introduced to him in a more dramatic manner.

Influenza was brought into the bay on a ship and was quickly spread throughout the community. Richard, who worked regularly with ship personnel, was infected and quarantined in a separate room in our home. Though we followed all the health department guidelines, it spread to the children and to me. Our house was quarantined. Jesse, who seemed to be immune, helped a team of health professionals who bravely visited quarantined houses, and he was present when Richard died. When my children also died, he visited me to offer assistance. At that time, it never occurred to me that he might be interested in me.

Our community lost a large portion of its population to the influenza which left vacancies in offices. Though women at that time were expected to be homemakers, I was able to get a job, thankfully, due to these vacancies, through Richard's associates at the government records office. Working there was difficult and stressful not only because I was inexperienced but also because the reduced staff couldn't handle the workload. Every day, the records office was filled with people waiting, impatiently, to be served. In addition to that, there was a movement to burn all the houses that were quarantined including my house that Richard and I had built after we married.

One evening, as I was eating alone, Jesse visited. I invited him to eat with me and he accepted. Asking me, like he does now, if anything needed repair, I broke into sobs about the demand to burn the house. As he knelt beside me to offer comfort and we were face-to-face, with a silent mutual agreement, our lips met. It was I who advanced the process as I got my hands under his shirt to feel his skin and follow the curves of his muscular chest. After that, he whispered my name, 'Beth', and the ravaging commenced. As we lay together, he invited me to stay with him, and suddenly, I didn't care what they did to my house.

Moving in with Jesse made me an outcast. People who once socialized with Richard and me, would not speak to me. Though the pastor who married Richard and me had died in the plague, his replacement never visited. My house along with contents was burned and I was able to sell the land giving me a little financial security, not that I needed it, I thought.

My first week in Jesse's house, Jesse made repairs, cut grass, walked to the wharf for supplies and I learned that he didn't like questions. He would not hear any question he didn't want to answer and, if I asked him again or a third time, he would leave. There was no show of emotion; he would just walk away from me until I could see him no more. I soon learned to be happy with whatever he wanted to share. I learned to observe when he took a second portion at a meal; I learned to notice what I was wearing when he smiled at me; I paid attention to anything that made him frown.

The first time Jesse left me to go to sea was a shock. The sun woke me as it peeked through the window and he was gone with no farewell. Standing in the dim kitchen, not knowing when he would return, I thought back to chaotic mornings with Richard and my children. I was longing for isolation then. I wept and felt sorry for myself for a long time. That's when I decided to look forward to Jesse's return with a vow to be ready for him whenever he appeared.

Chapter 2

When Jesse arrived from sea this time, he didn't fall into his chair and I was nowhere on his radar. Instead, he prepared a bath and didn't ask for my help. When he got dressed, in his nicest outfit, he left. As it got close to supper time, I prepared a meal like always, assuming Jesse would be at the table. To my amazement, a black carriage stopped at the front door. Jesse got out and, turning, he raised his hand to help a woman, who appeared to be younger than me, out of the carriage. She was wearing a dress of the latest fashion, light blue, puffy sleeves, ankle length skirt and matching bonnet.

Jesse escorted her into the house and introduced us; Kaylani was her name. Removing her bonnet revealed dark brown hair in a bun at the back of her head, skin touched by the sun and dark brown, almond-shaped eyes. 'Foreign' is the only way I could describe her with the knowledge I had of such things. Jesse brought in some bags followed by a man with a trunk then he asked if supper was ready so I led them to the table and set a third place.

Kaylani remarked that the food was delicious and said I should teach her the recipes. She said where she came from, they did not have a kitchen as nice as this.

"Where are you from?" I ventured to ask.

"What did you call it, Jesse?" Kaylani asked, smiling.

"Sandwich Islands," Jessie murmured, not looking up.

"Yes, Sandwich Islands," Kaylani repeated. "Isn't that something that we eat?"

She giggled at her reference not noticing that neither Jesse or I were laughing.

"I hope you will stay on," Kaylani continued.

"Stay on?" I stammered, looking at Jesse. "Was I going somewhere?"

Jesse rose and started to take steps toward the back door and I stood up.

"Don't walk away from this question, Jesse," I exclaimed.

Ignoring me, he continued walking but this time I followed, repeating the question. He was able to take larger strides than me but I trotted to keep up. Coming to a fence that marked the end of his property, he finally stopped.

"Kaylani is my wife," Jesse stated flatly, his back to me. "You're welcome to stay."

His words pierced my heart and sobs gushed out of the wound. As the will to live disappeared from my soul, I folded to the ground. True to his nature, Jesse walked away. After a while, I returned to the house to get my money. Jesse was in his chair. Walking into the bedroom that once was 'ours', Kaylani was unpacking, looking un-ravaged. Wondering if Jesse would be ravaging me now as his wife unpacked, I opened a box, pulled out a bag and left through the front door, heading down the hill I had once watched Jesse climb.

Knowing the wharf was not safe at night, I went to the police station. An officer on duty listened patiently as I explained I needed a place to stay. He very kindly expressed concern and told me of a rooming house close by. Telling his supervisor he was leaving, he escorted me to a two-story white house in a neighborhood of two-story white houses. An older lady, Edna, answered the door, even though it was late, and she did have a vacancy. Thanking the officer, he said good-night and Edna took me upstairs to a room barely large enough to accommodate a single bed. Putting my bag of money in a drawer, I lay down, wishing I were sleepy. As memories of my husband, children and Jesse tortured me, I rose to escape and headed toward the front door thinking I would sit on the porch. Passing a clock, it was between 3-4 AM. Like many of these homes, several chairs of various sorts were available on the porch. I chose a rocker where I could see the water and wondered if drowning was very painful. Too scared to pursue that path, I focused on the large ships anchored out in the deep part of the water and wondered about the Sandwich Islands and all the other places that ships sail to.

Hearing noises in the house, Edna opened the screen.

"Good morning," she greeted sincerely. "Are you an early riser like me?"

"Not really," I replied, glancing at her. "I couldn't sleep."

"Would you like some coffee?" she asked.

Following her down the dark hall into the kitchen, she put a cup on a small table for two and offered me the chair. The coffee smelled good and felt good going down. As I closed my eyes to relish the moment, sliced bread and butter with a small plate were placed on the table, followed by some simmering bacon. Edna, with silver hair in a bun, worked mechanically at the stove, concentrating on her tasks. Her plump figure filled out her blouse and ankle length skirt. Hearing her tenants coming down the stairs, she wished each of them a good morning. As she took plates of food into the dining room, which I couldn't see, I was grateful she let me stay in the kitchen with her. Eventually she brought a cup of coffee to the table, refilled my cup then sat down.

"I have to tell you that I checked on you this morning," she began looking worried. "Normally I don't check on tenants but coming in like you did with a police officer, I was concerned. Very few women in this community are on their own."

I didn't know how to respond to her statement. Actually, I hadn't figured out how to respond to this entire situation.

"You weren't in your room," she continued and pulled a key out of a pocket, "so I locked your door. Five men live in this house and sometimes things disappear. I've never caught any of them in the act but I will some day."

My money came to my mind and I wanted to go immediately to check it. When she informed me she had a safe I was welcome to use,

I expressed interest and she told me to bring my money to the table. We counted it and I mentioned that I needed clothes. She said she had clothes that no longer fit and we decided on an amount needed for undergarments. In a blank ledger book marked for me, she entered the rent paid, the remaining amount and I initialed it. If I had done the math correctly, I would be able to stay with Edna for a few years if needed. Sharing that with her, I offered to help her with care and maintenance of the house. She stared at me like I had offered her a fortune.

"You would do that for me?" she exclaimed.

"Of course," I responded flatly, seeing nothing wonderful about it. What else was I going to do anyway!

"In that case, your rent can be a little lower," she declared. "I gave up long ago looking for help. Most men don't want their wives or daughters in a house like this around five single men."

Hearing chairs scrape against the wood floor, we watched the men file out of the house. As Edna rose to enter the dining room, I followed. She explained that usually, the men were gone until supper. She picked up several dishes as I also did and, pouring hot water into the sink, she told me to bring the rest. As she washed, I pulled off the soiled table cloth, wiped off the chairs and swept the floor.

Chapter 3

The routine with Edna was comfortable and easy. Having managed two of my own households, her needs were obvious and she was grateful for everything I did. Though I never wanted to eat with the men, I did serve them breakfast and supper and got to know their names and anything about them they wanted to share. All of them were connected somehow to the shipping industry. Three of them were widowed and two, who were children during the plague, now, as young adults, were faced with a population of more men than women.

At night, I usually slept immediately having stayed physically active all day. One night, I was dreaming of a ravaging by Jesse and my body reacted as though it was real. My arm reached out to touch him and someone was actually there, on his knees beside my bed. In the darkness, I could not determine who it was and he dashed through the door. Scrambling out of the bed covers, I followed but the hall was empty and quiet. I locked my door at night, so this person evidently had a key. Unsure what to do, I knocked on Edna's door. Rather than letting me in, she came into the hall, a little unnerved.

"Are you hurt?" she asked but not with concern; more like a challenge.

"No," I answered and my voice elevated a little. "Someone has a key to my room! I'm not safe."

"Of course you're safe," Edna cooed. "No-one in this house would hurt you or anyone. I think I would know by now if anyone here was dangerous."

As her eyes begged me to believe her, curiosity grew in me about her room.

"Can't I stay with you?" I requested, just to get her reaction.

"Listen, Honey," she whispered. "I have a guest, actually."

"One of the men?" I asked, desperate to know.

"You have to be my friend on this, okay?" she implored. "I love his company; I don't want to lose it. I don't know what he would do if others found out."

"Which one?" I urged, bending close to her.

"Hal," she said with a smile as a gleam came into her eye.

Hal was probably the oldest of the men with thick silver hair and a rich, deep voice that was never irritated. He looked at people with a kindness in his eyes and a ready smile. Edna and I giggled and she embraced me.

Returning to my problem, I asked Edna if she had a different room I could use, which I knew she did. With a sigh, she disappeared into the bedroom and I heard soft talking. Coming out with her key ring, she walked to the last door in the hall and opened it to reveal another small room with a single bed. Giving me a key, she said good-night.

The next morning, as I served breakfast, I surveyed the five men in the dining room, assuming one of them was my late-night visitor. Except for Hal, all of them were suspects but none of them were acting suspicious. All of them were focused on their breakfast as usual and none of them acted differently in my presence. My visitor was either not at this table or he was an excellent actor.

Through the day, I pondered my visitor who evidently wanted so badly to ravage me he would risk being expelled from the rooming house. By the end of the day, I was calling him brave and wondered if he would visit again. Deciding to make it a challenge, though, I stayed in the last room in the hall and kept my night shirt unbuttoned.

A few days passed and, though I didn't stop anticipating his visit throughout the day, I became less observant when I laid down. As before, I fell asleep quickly. Finally, the ravaging dream occurred and, for some reason, I couldn't move my limbs. It was like they were locked in place. Fighting with my body for several minutes, I finally bolted up into a sitting position but my room was empty.

With disappointment, I lay back down, sighing.

"Beth," a man's voice whispered.

Opening my eyes, my visitor was knelt beside my bed. Wearing a black velvet robe with a hood made him hard to recognize.

"Are you alright?" he continued with concern.

Raising myself on my elbow to answer him, gravity pulled down my unbuttoned gown to reveal a breast. He smiled and gently caressed it, lightly touching the nipple, making a wave of arousal flow through my body.

"Did you unbutton this for me?" he asked playfully. "It is usually buttoned up tight."

"How many times have you been here?" I responded with wonder.

"Does it matter?" he replied as he slipped his lean, nude body under the covers.

Though his identity was secondary in my mind at this moment, it was one of the young men, Tyler. Unwrapping me like a precious gem, he did what he came to do and withdrew with no promise of return. It wasn't until the next morning, at the small kitchen table over coffee, that I considered the ramifications of this encounter. Unlike Richard and so much like Jesse, I had no commitment from Tyler. Jesse at least provided a home until he didn't want to. Tyler offered Tyler, maybe. Was I happy with this? Would Tyler be happy with a woman so much older? Remembering Richard's commitment, I realized what I had lost in the plague. To have a man caring about me, committed to me, and invested in me, was a priceless treasure. Tears fell onto the table and Edna came in.

Putting her arm on my shoulder she asked if I was alright. For the first time, I shared what happened to Richard and Jesse and now Tyler. After a while, I could see that my story was upsetting Edna. Reaching out to her, she shared that she also lost her husband in the plague but, thankfully, not her house. Her son, his wife and their two children sailed away to Great Britain; Edna opted to stay. Before he left, her son restructured the upstairs so that rental bedrooms were available.

My next encounter with Tyler began with a note on my bed to meet him at midnight in the back yard. As I exited the back door, it was very dark. I heard him approaching and he took my hand to lead me several yards away from the house. Edna's house was on a hill next to a woods which we entered. Eventually I heard flowing water and saw the soft glow of a fire in the distance. In front of a small tent was a blanket laying next to the fire. Tyler seated himself and gently pulled me beside him. Our lips met immediately, eagerly. While he quickly flung off his shirt, he seemed to like revealing my hidden parts slowly. I moved his hand to touch me where he hadn't before and he leaned his head back with eyes closed sighing deeply. Whispering that he was glad to know that was okay with me, he exclaimed that he knew something that I liked and he ravaged me with a vengeance.

Edna smiled knowingly as I entered the back door and mentioned she saw Tyler returning to the house. The glow of his attention and anticipation of future time with him stayed with me the entire day. To my delight, his visits became frequent and he often arranged something a little different. In the dining room, he smiled and winked at me constantly. One month, as I met with Edna to pay rent, she declared Tyler had paid it.

It was also gratifying that Tyler talked to me. He shared that his parents were taken in the plague as well as his brother; a neighbor took him in until he got a job on the wharf, starting as a wagon driver and moving to better paying positions with each year of experience. He hoped to have his own home someday, maybe working on the wharf or maybe farming; he wasn't sure and he wasn't concerned. He never talked about children or the difference in our ages.

As if his attentions and his arrangements did not delight me enough, he managed a surprise for me that I'll never forget. Some of the tasks I did for Edna involved walking to the wharf for chores like retrieving mail or picking up special items. These were not daily trips so

I have no idea how Tyler managed to be waiting for me. Walking up to me as though we were strangers, he greeted me.

"Good day, Ma'am," he began. "Let me introduce myself, Tyler Houston."

With giggles at his playfulness and the surprise of his appearance, I played along beginning with a curtsey.

"So nice to meet you, Mr. Houston," I replied with a coy smile.

"Pardon my boldness, Ma'am," he droned. "Being such a thing of beauty, I must ask you, would you dine with me tonight?"

"Oh!" I exclaimed. "You are incorrigible, Mr. Houston."

He then took my hand and led me to a waiting carriage and we left our small community. It had been years since I had been driven away from that little town. In a short time, we walked into a restaurant. As the food was served, he left me for a few minutes then returned. After enjoying the wonderful meal and conversation, he led me to a different part of the building where he stopped at a counter and gave his name. The clerk handed him a key and said everything was prepared.

Stepping into a nice sized room, with a beautifully carved wooden bed, he escorted me to a bathing room where a steaming bath was waiting. Walking to the windows, instead of closing them, he pushed back curtains and blinds to let in as much light as possible.

"I want you to wash me," he whispered as he removed his clothing. "I've been wanting this for such a long time. I want you to be very thorough."

Rather than getting into the tub, he stood outside it and handed me a sponge that he lathered with soap. Seeing him in ecstasy, I wanted to give him exactly what he asked for. With myself fully clothed, I covered every inch of his body with my hands, not the sponge, paying attention to those places that seemed to give him the most pleasure. He then slipped into the tub, asked me to join him and he washed me thoroughly. When I was rinsed off, he carried me to the bed for a ravaging.

Chapter 4

I should know by now that achieving contentment would at some point coast into despair. The descent began with the arrival of Edna's granddaughter, which was expected and Edna was very excited. Asking me to meet her, I walked to the wharf. Having the name of the ship she was on, one of the wharfsmen pointed to it's location in the deep water. He said passengers were now being rowed to the dock. As row boats arrived, I was relieved to see a young woman in a puffy-sleeved white and yellow ankle-length dress with a yellow bonnet accompanied by a child two or three years old. Walking toward her, I asked if she was Sarah Hartman and she was. The child was a girl, Rebecca or Becky. We found an available carriage and the driver retrieved Sarah's luggage.

The two travelers were obviously tired, maybe sick, as they stayed quiet during the short trip to the rooming house. Edna bounded out of the house to greet Sarah with a hug and crooned over the child, who started to cry. The driver put Sarah's luggage on the sidewalk but no further. It was going to have to stay there until one of the men got home. By the time I got in the house, Sarah, the child and Edna were upstairs. At this point, Sarah's arrival was a distraction, nothing more. Busying myself with dusting and entertaining my brain with fantasies of Tyler, it came to be supper time when Edna reappeared to start cooking. A few of the men came in carrying the luggage; they set it in the hall then they went on the porch to wait for supper.

With a tray prepared for Sarah, Edna asked me to take it upstairs. Happy to help, I knocked on the door and Sarah asked who I was. Answering I had a tray of food, she said to come in. Balancing the tray to open the door, with some fear it would spill, I walked into the dark room. Sarah pointed where she wanted it. Becky was asleep and Sarah was laying on a lounge in her undergarments; she didn't look at me or speak. Unlike my single bed, a wooden double bed with canopy took up half of the room; the rest of it was occupied with a writing desk, a wardrobe, chest of drawers and a large fireplace. Returning to Edna, she asked if Sarah was alright and I told her what I saw: that she was laying on the lounge and Becky was asleep. Sarah then appeared in the kitchen in her undergarments.

"Sarah! There are male tenants here," Edna scolded.

"I need my luggage," Sarah whined. "I need a bath."

Edna walked out of the kitchen to lead Sarah back to her room. I felt the first downward tug of despair as Tyler walked through the front door and Edna asked him to take Sarah's luggage upstairs. As Sarah passed him, the look of intense interest on Tyler's face plunged through my heart like a dagger. To my relief though, Tyler visited me that night and restored some level of contentment. As the days passed and Sarah became a permanent part of the household's routine, it was apparent to me that Sarah was brought up to flatter and pander to men; and didn't they love it.

I watched with interest as Sarah built a social life, something I never did because I was born here, I suppose and, being married to Richard, we associated with families he knew. Sarah made formal visits to people who knew Edna and left her calling card. This resulted in them visiting her which required making tea and cookies and also stocking wine and liquor.

On one occasion, Sarah was invited to a ball given by leaders of the community and she asked Tyler to escort her. On the night of the ball, I took a blanket to the woods where Tyler had pitched that tent and bawled for hours. The next morning, Tyler's behavior toward me had not changed - still smiling, still winking - and I was relieved. Because of that, the next ball and ensuing balls were not as threatening. My contentment level remained steady as he acknowledged and visited me as he had for over a year.

The day Sarah's engagement to Tyler was published was the day a piece of my heart was cut from my chest. Telling Edna I was ill, I stayed in my room. Picturing the beautiful hours Tyler and I had spent together only putting Sarah's image in my place sent waves of pain over my entire body. I kissed the pillow where Tyler had laid his head and caressed the sheet he had laid on. Later than night, he visited me, kneeling beside me as usual until I woke up. I rejected his advances and sat up.

"What are you doing?" I cried.

"I was afraid you would respond like this," he answered. "I was hoping you wouldn't."

"What did you expect, exactly?" I challenged.

"No change in our relationship," he stated flatly. "Why does it have to change?"

"Why are you marrying her?" I wailed, as tears now escaped.

He sat close beside me with his arm behind me.

"She has built impressive connections," he explained. "I've been given an important position. She needs a husband to bring in an income. That's all she wants from me."

"You won't sleep with her?" I hoped.

"I won't enjoy it," he responded and I turned from him. "Women like that don't want what we have. Whether she knows it or not, I'm the perfect choice for her kind."

He put his mouth close to my ear.

"Beth," he whispered.

Somehow he knew I loved hearing my name and I relented to one of the best ravagings ever. In our afterglow, he promised he would meet me at midnight often and he would take me out of here to our own place. I chose to believe in him and fell asleep in his arms.

On Sarah's wedding day, Sarah was in her room surrounded by her bridesmaids to help her dress. At Edna's bidding, I was in the room. I guess Edna thought I would enjoy the pre-wedding ritual. A full length mirror was in the middle of the room and Sarah took off her robe to stand nude before us. Knowing Tyler would be experiencing her young, vibrant body made me lose strength and I excused myself. Again, I went to the creek for solace and Tyler was sitting there.

Hearing me, he stood then rushed to me as I did to him. In my life so far, I had never been engulfed in a man's arms like he was engulfing me. He cupped my chin but didn't kiss me.

"We have to be strong, Beth," he warned. "As hard as this is, it is the best for us."

"This is torture for you," I observed seeing the stress in his face. "Are you sure it is the best?"

"A man like me will never have an opportunity like this," he answered. "I'll be surrounded by men who know how to build wealth."

"Tyler, we have been happy this last year without wealth, haven't we?" I suggested.

"We get a taste of happiness now and again," he responded. "Just a taste. I can make myself go to work every day but the meager earnings go into Edna's safe. The owners who pay my wages have continual happiness. This is my chance, our chance, to move to that level."

Pulling out his pocket watch he looked at the time and said he wanted me to wash him as he disrobed and walked into the creek. Taking off my shoes and socks, I scooped water into my cupped hands and rubbed his body as though I were soaping him. The water was cold and he started to shiver but he insisted we continue. Then as he reached for me, I playfully ran from him. Bringing me down, he covered my head with my skirt, pulled down my bloomers and shared himself with me.

"Now I'm ready," he said uncovering my face. "I should have said this to you a hundred times: you have sustained me this last year and you sustained me today. All day, I will remember that you washed every part of me. All day, Beth, and all night."

To my amazement that night, his wedding night, I woke to Tyler kneeling beside me, although he wasn't in his velvet robe. Without disrobing, he slipped under the covers.

"I did my duty," he whispered. "I was able to perform for her."

His eyes were closed as he spoke and he was hot with fever. He nuzzled close to me, laying his arm across my chest, breathing softly. Looking at him, cherishing him, stroking his hair, his arm went limp; his breathing stopped. My descent to despair gained speed, entering blackness.

Chapter 5

In one of the row boats, I watched my community shrink in size as the distance between me and the shore widened. Tyler's death in my bed ignited a scandal the community relished. Though Edna was faulted for allowing the affair in her rooming house, she rarely left the house so she never heard anything said about her. Sarah, as the victim, became a hero of sorts as she bravely received guests. She managed to look stunning in the black wardrobe she chose. Given the number of males who called on her, it would be no time at all before she married again. For me, the rooming house was a torture chamber. Tyler was in every room. Tyler was in the back yard and at the creek. My longing for him was constant. It was Edna who suggested that I sail to Great Britain where her son lived.

In the Great Britain port city, I was able to leave the ship directly onto the wharf. Seeing a man who looked like a police officer, I asked for directions on the envelope Edna had given me. He said it was a far walk and suggested a cab. Telling him how much money I had, he clicked his teeth and said he would walk with me aways. As we met up with another officer, he was told the destination and I walked with him a while. After walking with another two officers, I reached the address; quite tired. Knocking on the door, a woman, a little older than me, answered. Handing her the letter, she led me to a parlor where I could sit.

The next thing I knew, I woke in a small room lying on a single bed, still in the same clothes, very hungry and needing a lavatory. Opening the door and looking right, the hall led to a back door; looking left led to a kitchen. Seeing no-one, I turned right and found an outhouse. Walking back to the kitchen, I pumped a little water to wash off my hands. The noise brought in the same woman who had greeted me the night before.

"How are you, Beth?" she asked.

"Thank you for asking, Ma'am," I answered. "I'm hungry, if you don't mind. I have a little money."

"I'm sure you are," the woman agreed as she moved into the kitchen. "Travel by ship isn't easy and you walked from the pier, am I right?"

"Yes, Ma'am," I answered.

The gracious, slender lady wore a starched white blouse and light green ankle-length skirt, tight at the waist then broadening at the hem. Her brown hair showing some gray was bound in a bun on top of her head. Motioning me to have a seat at the table, she set down a plate of bread and a jar of jam.

"I'm Clarissa Rogers and you probably know I am Edna's daughter-in-law," she stated. "Will you have coffee?"

"Yes, Ma'am, thank you," I answered.

Setting down a cup of coffee with one for herself, she sat across from me.

"Edna said you have experienced a lot of tragedy in your young life," Clarissa said.

"A little happiness," I responded thinking of Tyler, though I knew my face reflected sadness at his memory.

"That's a good perspective," Clarissa complimented. "Focus on the blessings?"

"Yes, Ma'am," I replied as I started to weep.

Clarissa rushed to comfort me and she let me weep for several minutes.

"You're tired, burnt out," Clarissa soothed as she rocked me gently then she whispered. "Dear Lord, please help Beth."

At that moment, I realized it had been years since I heard a prayer. My parents took us to church as children; Richard and I attended church, but, like I said, I was an outcast when I moved in with Jesse, ignored by the new minister.

Leaning back from Clarissa, wide-eyed, at this woman who prayed, she asked me if I wanted to bathe. Telling her I did, she showed me the tub with towels and cloths which was close by. She pumped water into a couple of kettles and led me to stacks of wood. Then, telling me she would be upstairs at the first door on the right, she left me to take care of myself.

Taking my time, I soaked a little and wept a little remembering Tyler's love of being washed. Unbundling my clothes and hanging them on pegs, I ventured, with a sigh, up the stairs to find Clarissa. She was seated in the room on the right with glasses on, writing. When I knocked gently, she removed her glasses and motioned to a chair.

"How can we help you, Beth?" she asked.

"I need a job, a place to stay." I answered.

"Would that little room downstairs be alright?" she asked.

"Yes, Ma'am," I replied with relief.

"We are looking for a cook," she began.

"I can cook, Ma'am," I answered with confidence. "I can clean if you like."

Offering me a wage I thought was generous, she gave me a pen and paper and asked for a menu for the rest of the week, three days. Asking her if there were dislikes, she mentioned a few. Asking her how much I could spend, she gave me a range. Going to the kitchen and taking inventory, I returned shortly with my suggestions. When she ask the cost and I told her everything was on hand, she laughed with delight.

"My Precious Beth," she cried. "I'm praising God for you."

That night Clarissa presented me to her husband, Gordon, a tall lean man with a structured jaw and intense blue eyes. Though he welcomed me sincerely with a smile, he asked his wife a question then bounded up the stairs. Telling me he would be out for the evening, Clarissa said supper would be required for the two of us.

As we ate together, which I thought was unusual in homes who hired servants, I asked what Gordon did and she explained he worked in a government office that tended to be political and it occupied most of his time. Then I asked about her son, whose name was Riley. It was Clarissa's turn to sigh and be sad because he had picked up gambling, a prominent past time in their city, and it was destroying him. Right now he was staying with wealthy friends he met at school, making a little money here and there then gambling it away.

"You knew my daughter, of course," Clarissa stated.

"Yes, Ma'am," I answered as I stiffened with apprehension.

"She also has experienced a measure of tragedy," Clarissa murmured.

Clearing my throat and shifting a little, I hoped she would not mention Tyler.

"Sarah was married before," I said.

"Yes," Clarissa acknowledged with a nod. "He died of heart failure."

Clarissa looked away like she was replaying some past scene and went on to explain: Sarah's husband's debts left Sarah penniless forcing her to move in with Clarissa and Gordon, and, Sarah hated being a dependent. She also hated being in mourning and being penniless. When a letter arrived from Edna, it gave Sarah the idea to travel there.

"Hearing that her second husband, a young man, also died was heartbreaking," Clarissa mourned. "How was she when you left?"

Picturing the male visitors who flocked to visit Sarah, I searched for words Clarissa might want to hear.

"She's handling it as well as one would expect," I said. "Becky is a delight, to be sure. Edna adores her."

Clarissa sighed and, when the doorbell rang, she rose to answer it. I cleared the table and washed the dishes. Clarissa didn't return to the kitchen.

The next morning as I was taking inventory with the intention of shopping, the door bell rang. A gruff sounding man spoke to Clarissa and I heard him stomp up the stairs. Then, to my horror, I heard Sarah. Frozen for a moment, I grabbed my purse and bonnet and rushed out the back door to the shops. Managing to stay away for a few hours, I returned through the back entrance. The noises I made putting items away brought Clarissa into the kitchen to tell me that Sarah had arrived and Gordon would be home at 8 PM for supper. I nodded when she asked me if this was alright then I asked about Becky. Clarissa said Becky was with Edna.

Picturing an encounter with Sarah was terrifying, assuming I would be expelled because her husband had died in my bed. My plans to clean the rooms upstairs quickly changed to scrubbing the downstairs. At 6 PM, I started cooking. At 7:30, with severe anxiety, I went to the dining room to set the table. At 7:55, I put plates of food into a dumbwaiter and walked upstairs. Clarissa met me and helped set food on the table.

"You aren't joining us?" Clarissa said with surprise.

Her question was a shock, a delightful shock actually, and I let out a little laugh.

"Thank you, Ma'am," I said smiling. "So kind of you to ask. I'll let you have private time with Sarah, alright?"

Clarissa nodded also smiling now and I set myself a plate on the table in the kitchen. Not much conversation was coming out of the dining room and I wondered if Sarah had even come down. Then I heard her wailing like she had that day in Edna's kitchen when she wanted a bath. Shortly after, chairs scraped on the wood floor and conversation stopped. Minutes later, the dumbwaiter was lowered; Clarissa had cleared the table. Rising to empty the dumbwaiter, Clarissa appeared with the soiled table cloth and took it to the laundry bin. Then, retrieving a fresh table cloth, she left. I marveled how different she was from other wealthy women who had servants for these tasks. Knowing the upstairs needed to be dusted and swept and wanting it to be done for Clarissa, I vowed to resolve this issue with Sarah. My opportunity came the next morning when Sarah appeared in the kitchen for coffee. I stood before her waiting for her reaction.

"Beth," she seethed, her eyes squinting at me.

"Sarah," I answered trying to remain calm.

"Would you pour me a coffee?" she asked, sitting down. "Join me, won't you."

I sat across from her.

"I wondered if I would see you though I didn't expect my parents to hire you," she laughed. "Life is so...unpredictable, isn't it."

Before I could answer, she continued.

"Tyler's infidelity wasn't so much of a shock as who he was unfaithful with," Sarah murmured. "Are you twenty years older? The body grows flabby at your age, does it not?"

Seeing Sarah's cruel, sadistic nature made me happy for Tyler knowing he would never experience her behavior. In spite of her desire to torture me, she actually freed me from my grief for him. So many things I could have said to her about his love and desire for me; about his reason for marrying her; and his plans for me, but I wanted this encounter to be over, not prolonged. Seeing that I wasn't responding to her question, she tried again.

"I'm carrying his baby," she hissed, then she put the coffee cup to her lips and looked at me over the rim.

I'm sure she was delighted when I shot back in my chair with my eyes closed feeling an ache in my heart that should have killed me. She then rose, satisfied with the wound she inflicted and slowly walked by me close enough to brush against me. In a disturbing way, rather than being expelled, I knew she would keep me on just so she could torture me. Finishing my coffee, I took broom, dust mop and dust cloth upstairs. Clarissa was in her office and Sarah joined her.

"I got a response from the doctor," Sarah said to Clarissa. "This is how much he wants."

"We told you last night, we won't pay for an abortion," Clarissa answered firmly. "Regardless of the circumstances, the baby is a gift from God."

"You hired his hoar, Mother!" Sarah shouted. "Do you know what you're asking? I have to give birth to his baby and live with his hoar? How much do you think I can stand!"

The next sound was Sarah's footsteps running up the stairs. Clarissa appeared saying she wanted to talk to me.

"How much did you hear?" she asked and I repeated what I heard.

"Were you Tyler's...?" Clarissa began.

"Yes, Ma'am," I interrupted with a little defiance. No way was I going to be ashamed. "Though I would not use that word. We loved each other."

"Why weren't you married then?" Clarissa asked with complete innocence. It was obvious that love and marriage went together in her mind.

I myself had pondered this question many times and I regret now that I never asked Tyler to find out his reasons.

"I believe he had a vision of what he wanted for me but he didn't have the means," I offered and I continued with my next statement knowing it would be hurtful to Clarissa. "He believed that marrying Sarah would make him wealthy."

"And..." Clarissa said looking at me with fear in her eyes, "he was going to use that wealth..."

"To find a place for us, yes," I answered for her, seeing her cringe.

Bringing her hands together as though she were praying, she closed her eyes for almost a minute then she rose stating she would have to talk to Gordon. After supper that night, at the dining room table, Clarissa asked me to join her and Gordon. Gordon rose when I entered and greeted me with a smile.

"Are you familiar with sin, Beth?" Gordon began in a tone I would expect from a teacher.

"Yes, Sir," I answered remembering the years of church I had attended.

"What about adultery and fornication?" he continued.

" 'Thou shat not commit adultery'[1]," I responded repeating the well-known commandment.

"And fornication?" he pressed.

I had no answer for him; he explained.

"God designed sex to be shared between a man and a woman who are committed to building a family," Gordon stated. "Sex shared outside that union is either adultery or fornication in God's eyes."

Looking at me intensely he asked if I understood. I nodded that I did.

"So, do you see how the Bible describes your behavior?" Gordon asked.

I nodded, feeling uncomfortable at this comparison. Clarissa was looking at me with compassion.

"Now, do you know about the woman caught in adultery?" Gordon continued but not waiting for my answer, he turned to his Bible.

"John chapter 8[2], verse 3: 'And the scribes and Pharisees brought unto him (Jesus) a woman taken in adultery...',

then in verse 7, Jesus said, 'He that is without sin among you, let him first cast a stone at her.'

and finally in verses 10 and 11, Jesus said, 'Woman, where are those thine accusers? hath no man condemned thee? She said, No man, Lord. And Jesus said unto her, Neither do I condemn thee: go, and sin no more."

Gordon leaned forward.

"You may not fully understand what Jesus did for that woman," Gordon began, "but Clarissa and I are going to follow what Jesus did. Clarissa and I do not condemn your past behavior, Beth, but can you turn from that behavior?"

With no immediate answer from me, Gordon tried again.

"In other words, can you abstain from sex until you are married with God's blessing?" he asked.

"May I speak to Clarissa?" I requested.

Gordon rose with a nod and a smile and touched Clarissa's shoulder as he passed. Clarissa moved closer to me.

"I value what you are doing," I started, "and I know most people would just fire me so I want to be honest with you. I have no physical desires right now. My love for Tyler didn't die with him. But my love for Richard didn't stop my love for Jesse and my love for Jesse didn't stop my love for Tyler. I mean, if I meet someone else..."

"Let's leave it like this," Clarissa proposed. "Tell me if you meet someone, alright? Before you get involved, please?"

Chapter 6

Sarah made sure her outrage at her pregnancy inflicted everyone but she especially loved scathing me at every opportunity. Though I dusted and swept every room, I tried to wait to clean her room when she was gone, but she put a stop to that by demanding that I clean when she was there. One time, she chose to undress in my presence and, fondling her enlarged breasts, she commented that she was sorry Tyler never got to enjoy them. She stated that he loved bathing her on their wedding night and he ravaged her for hours, multiple times. I knew that wasn't true, given his condition when he climbed into my bed. Knowing she wanted a cat fight, however, I kept comments to myself.

How I had the stamina, during Sarah's term, to endure her cruelty was a mystery to me. In her last month, she was bedridden but, in my estimation, it was out of pity for herself, not out of physical weakness. Her demands on me became so frequent, Clarissa or I often sat in her room waiting for the next summons. At one of the doctor's visits, he recommended, to my dismay, that we give her massages. Clarissa asked me to purchase the lotion, which I did, knowing I would have to apply it. It probably makes God chuckle that, after all the tragedies in my life, this little task made me humble myself before him. I asked him to give me strength to massage Sarah.

So after Clarissa bathed Sarah one day with my help because Sarah was too heavy to lower and lift into the tub, Sarah laid on the lounge waiting for her massage. Glaring at me with squinted eyes, I knew she was preparing a barrage of references to Tyler touching her. To my amazement, Clarissa walked out of the tub room and asked me to clean it up. With a smile of relief, I handed the lotion to Clarissa, looked up to God and thanked him.

Clarissa and I were spared future massages as Sarah went into labor and was transported to a hospital. A little girl, Lorelai Houston, was born. I knew ladies in Sarah's social class stayed in the hospital for a week if not longer and I cherished every quiet moment. Lorelei's arrival was greatly anticipated by Gordon and Clarissa but for me, I was expecting her to be a painful reminder of Tyler's absence. Within moments of her arrival, I was thrust into that gauntlet because Sarah wanted nothing to do with the baby. Lorelai was crying as she was brought into the house - time for a breastfeeding. It was only with Clarissa's firm insistence that Sarah offered one of her breasts and she refused to hold onto the child. I sat on the bed and held the baby. When Lorelai was done, at Sarah's insistence, we left the bedroom.

In the nursery, I laid the baby in her crib and studied her, looking for signs of Tyler. But nothing appeared. Instead, by the grace of God perhaps, I saw the tiny, vulnerable human totally dependent on the adults in her life. She had no way of knowing that her mother's rejection was a blessing because instead of being scorned, she would be loved by her grandparents and perhaps by me. And I wouldn't love her because she was Tyler but because Tyler, had he lived, would want me to care for her. More than that, in my infant relationship with God, I knew he would want me to care for his new creation.

To ease his wife's distress over Sarah's behavior, Gordon made a deal with Sarah to breastfeed the baby, peacefully, until she is weaned and he would pay Sarah's passage back to Edna. When she insisted on an allowance, he agreed if every breastfeeding was peaceful and until she was married. The following year was torture for Sarah and she struggled to withhold her hatred of the child to gain passage away from it. In between feedings, she fussed at her figure working to restore her girlish looks and scoured clothing magazines for the latest fashion. Every allowance bought her a new item for her trunk. When Lorelai was eleven months old, Sarah boarded a ship to Edna's.

Chapter 7

My status, after Sarah's departure, became an unofficial adopted family member and I was moved into Sarah's room, next to the nursery. Although Clarissa wanted to hire a cook and housekeeper, I insisted that she let me manage those things. It became a running joke when Clarissa would playfully suggest someone for cook and I would rage at her for making such a silly suggestion. True to scripture, Clarissa, with other church friends, visited widows and orphans[3]. Not only did I join their church, but I understood that God wanted me to follow his lead as prescribed in the Bible, and he wanted me to cherish Jesus who made himself the permanent sacrifice for the damage done 'to me' when sin entered the world[4]. Many people don't understand their condition in God's eyes and I can only pray that you will ask God about it.

When Lorelai was two years old, it was decided she needed a new bed. Clarissa, Lorelai and I visited some furniture shops and some country carpenter shops. At one of the carpenter shops, we were assisted by Jonathan, who would have been Richard's age had he lived. A sturdy, yet agile man, not much taller than me, his light hair, brushed away from his forehead, was streaked with gray; his eyes were a deep ocean green and his smile welcoming. Liking one of his beds, Clarissa arranged for it to be delivered.

When Clarissa opened the door the next day, Jonathan had arrived with a helper; I was in the kitchen and I heard them arrive. The pieces of the bed, in their wagon, were carried to Lorelei's room to be assembled. They worked for twenty or thirty minutes and notified Clarissa that a piece had been left at the shop so they had to return. Being after the noon hour already, Jonathan returned by himself to finish the bed and Clarissa invited him to supper. With humble gratitude, he accepted the invitation. Clarissa showed Jonathan where to sit, which was next to me. To our delight, Jonathan offered to say grace.

Clarissa began the conversation and I question to this day if she said this on purpose.

"You're wife doesn't have supper waiting for you?" Clarissa asked with concern.

"I'm a widow, Ma'am," Jonathan answered. "Been without my wife almost twenty years."

"I'm so sorry," Clarissa consoled. "Were you blessed with children?"

"We were, Ma'am," Jonathan smiled. "One you met today. He'll likely take over the shop in a few years. A girl is married living in another state and another boy is in the military."

"Grandchildren then?" Clarissa pressed.

"Yes, Ma'am," Jonathan smiled, "that I haven't got to meet though. The shop keeps us busy."

"You offered grace, Jonathan," Clarissa stated, "to my delight. Are you Christian?"

"Born-again, Ma'am," Jonathan answered quickly. "Dedicated to my Savior."

Clarissa and I looked at each other with a smile. It was always a joy to meet a fellow believer. This then prompted Jonathan to describe his encounter with Jesus.

"Though it's been a few years, I wish for my family's sake it had been sooner," Jonathan remarked. "I could have loved them better; treated them better."

"Amen," I said agreeing, feeling warmth in my face then I admitted. "I'm very new at loving Jesus."

"Welcome to the family, My Sister," Jonathan replied with a smile. "Jesus accepts us at all stages, doesn't he? Even the great Apostle Paul agreed to murder[5] before he met Jesus[6]!"

In a few weeks, Jonathan appeared at the door again wanting to speak to me. He said I had been on his mind and wondered if we could go to dinner. Remembering the promise I made to Clarissa, I excused myself and went to her, upstairs. She said to invite him to church and Sunday dinner, which I did and he accepted. At Sunday dinner, Gordon and Jonathan discussed scripture and a little politics. As Jonathan rose to leave, I accompanied him to the door and Clarissa joined us.

"I see you're doing this old-school," Jonathan said to Clarissa. "This girl must be very special to you."

"She's special to God," Clarissa answered.

My heart warmed at her statement making me smile.

"You're blessed, Beth," Jonathan stated and left.

Jonathan attended church and Sunday dinner for the rest of the year. After a New Year's Eve church service, the congregation remained to fellowship. Jonathan led the pastor, me, Clarissa, Gordon and Lorilai to some seats where Jonathan could speak to all of us.

"It is settled in my mind and heart," Jonathan began, "that I'd like to take Beth as my wife. This is the first she's heard of this though, being a smart woman, she probably isn't surprised."

I laughed softly looking down, shaking my head slowly.

"I do have a knack for picking the smart ones, Pastor," Jonathan joked, then he got serious. "With the care you have taken to protect Beth, which I applaud, I do have some private things to say to her. Can that be arranged?"

"This is the perfect place," Gordon stated and we agreed.

With everyone stepping away from Jonathan and me, he gave me his full attention.

"I think we like each other, Beth," Jonathan began. "I've seen you take care of your family and I want that in my life. Would you want to take care of me and my house."

"I would want to," I answered softly.

"You've seen my place and my shop," Jonathan continued. "Would you want to live there?"

"Yes, I would want to live there," I answered.

"One last thing," he said and he shifted with some discomfort. "After my wife died, I did some things that I'm ashamed of; things I will share with you in private, confidentially. It wasn't murder or stealing or rape, nothing like that. I didn't hurt nobody except for myself. But, I turned from that stuff when I found Jesus. I turned from it, alright? Can you believe in me?"

I loved the sincerity in his face and I wanted to touch him.

"I have things to share, too," I responded. "One of the things involves Lorelai's father and it haunts me, Jonathan. I pray for it to be gone, but it remains. Can you accept me on that basis?"

"I bet my secret is more horrible than yours," he whispered.

Rising from his chair, he took my hand and led me to the pastor, Gordon, Clarissa and Lorelai asking when they could get us married. With cries of joy, Clarissa embraced me and the men shook hands. They set the date.

On our wedding night, Jonathan put blankets, pillows and provisions in the wagon and we drove to the highest hill on his property. A campsite was there indicating it was a spot visited frequently. The sun was low in the west but not yet at the horizon. Sitting close next to a fire, Jonathan shared his secrets and they were pretty bad; shocking even. He wept with remorse. Though I shared Richard's death and my experience with Jesse, it was Tyler's love and Tyler's death that haunted me; torturing me, like a cancer in my heart.

"I'm sensing a deep wound, Beth," Jonathan said, "Wounds like that...wounds like that may not heal."

He drew me close and looked at the setting sun.

"I'm praying for God to help you," he whispered.

He stretched out on the blanket and, when I laid beside him, he wrapped himself around me, gently rubbing my back; I slept and I dreamed about Jesus.

"Beth," Jesus said. "If Tyler had been following me, what would have happened?"

"He would have married me," I answered.

"Would marrying you guarantee that he would be alive today?" Jesus asked.

"No," I whispered with sadness.

"Physical death is inevitable, is it not?" Jesus asked.

"It is inevitable," I repeated.

"Death took Richard and Death took Tyler," Jesus stated. "I see no difference in their departures from this earth, except you aren't letting go of Tyler. He doesn't belong to this earth anymore; he doesn't belong to you. He belongs to me and my Father."

Jesus continued.

"You belong to us as well, Beth," he stated. "I've sent Jonathan to you. Bless him and you will be blessed."

My eyes opened with the sun pushing back the darkness. Sitting up slowly, not wanting to disturb Jonathan, I saw a creek at the bottom of the hill. In a few minutes, he sat up beside me and drew me close. Then I stood up.

"Is there a good bathing spot in that creek?" I asked.

He shot up cheering, "Oh, Yeah!", and we raced to the creek where we blessed each other as God designed. Now I praise God that he gave me a man who cares about me, who is committed to me and who is invested in me...he is a priceless treasure.

Book 2 - Chapter 1

Clarissa sat in her office chair with two letters, one from Beth and one from Edna. Reading Beth's first, Clarissa was delighted that Beth was happy and content with Jonathan, and Beth urged Clarissa to visit. Then, reading Edna's letter, Clarissa sat back in her chair and looked to Heaven for guidance. It said Sarah was ill and Clarissa wanted to go to her. It occurred to her that maybe she could get her son, Riley, to join her and get him away from the casinos. Clarissa wondered often how her two children, raised on the Bible and basked in prayer, could have chosen God-less lives. At the same time, she knew the answer, 'God didn't create robots'.

At the supper table with Gordon that night, Clarissa read Beth's letter and then Edna's. His face was grim as Clarissa shared a desire to go to Sarah and take Riley.

"I love that you want to go to her," Gordon began. "I'd prefer to go with you but, of course, I can't."

"You will agree to my going then?" Clarissa asked with hope.

"With great concern," he answered taking her hand. "Let me find the best voyage. How will you contact Riley?"

"Actually, I know where he will be this weekend because one of his friends is getting married," Clarissa answered. "The wedding announcement was published."

"You won't have time to write him," Gordon observed.

"No, I'll have to travel there," Clarissa responded. "I could spend the night with Beth."

"A night without you in my bed?" Gordon teased. "Now you are asking too much."

Clarissa stood up and put her face close to his.

"You better get it while you can, Sir," she whispered and turned away from him.

When he rose from the table, she rushed from his grasp, giggling as she ran up the stairs. He bounded after her.

The next day, after several hour's drive, Clarissa's carriage approached the vintage manor house. Surveying the manicured gardens on either side of the long lane, Clarissa marveled that anyone could afford the upkeep and add to that, the manor itself that was three times larger than her home.

When she was shown into the house, her eyes first fell on a grand staircase almost as wide as she was tall, with light walnut railings and burgundy carpet. She was led into a parlor and offered tea. It was a while before the housekeeper came in with apologies that the manor's master and mistress were not home. Telling the housekeeper she wanted to see Riley, the housekeeper folded her hands with a look of worry and excused herself. The next person to appear was a gardener or stableman, Clarissa wasn't sure, but she followed him when beckoned. Being led to a room in the stable, she walked next to a single bed to see her son lying there, covered with a coarse blanket and smelling really bad. Putting her hand on his shoulder, he turned over and Clarissa gasped in shock. Riley's eyes were black, with a cut on his forehead and his mouth was swollen.

"Mother," Riley said the best he could through his swollen lips.

Clarissa sat on the bed and, as he turned toward her, she saw his white shirt was streaked with blood. Seeing his mother's distressed expression, Riley offered an explanation.

"I had to pay on a gambling debt," he explained as he tried to chuckle, "with my face. You should see the other guy."

"Riley," was all Clarissa could say as her face puckered to fight tears.

"What's wrong?" Riley asked sitting up with a sigh. "Is Father alright?"

"Yes, yes, he's fine," Clarissa answered. "Sarah is ill and she is with Edna. I want to go to her."

"The Princess," Riley responded shaking his head. "We have been summoned."

As Clarissa and Riley walked toward Edna's front door, the men on the porch watched with interest. Edna rarely got visitors, especially gracious, beautiful women like Clarissa. When Edna saw Clarissa through the screen door, she let out a squeal of delight and rushed to her. Becky, now five years old, popped out of the sitting room with curiosity.

"My baby is home," Edna murmured as she embraced Clarissa. Then turning to Becky, "This is your grandmother."

"Aren't you my grandmother?" Becky asked Edna, looking confused.

"I am your great-grandmother," Edna instructed. "And this is Riley?"

"None other," Riley acknowledged with a wide smile.

"Your Uncle Riley," Edna said to Becky. "Sarah's brother."

"Is Sarah here?" Clarissa asked with worry.

"She is bedridden in her home," Edna answered. "But it's nearly time for supper. Won't you eat with us. I've got your room ready and the men will carry your luggage."

By the time supper was done and Clarissa helped clean up, she was ready to rest for the night. Edna showed her to the bedroom Sarah had occupied years ago. Riley was shown a room with a single bed.

The next morning, the hired carriage transported Clarissa with an overnight bag up the hill toward Jesse's house then past the cemetery where Tyler was laid and past the land once owned by Beth and Richard. It should not have shocked Clarissa that Sarah married a man who could own a manor similar to the one where she found Riley. A servant led Clarissa into a parlor then she was soon joined by Sarah's husband, Monty, who was a head shorter than Clarissa, probably ten years older, wearing a gray suit with vest tailored to accommodate his round Santa belly. Speaking softly in worried tones, he thanked Clarissa for coming, asked her if she needed refreshments then led her up the grand staircase to Sarah's room.

Actually, it wasn't a room, but a suite. Sarah's oversized bed in the center of the suite, was flanked by a full-sized desk one would expect to find in an executive's office and by a sitting area with several comfortable chairs in front of a massive fireplace. When Clarissa saw her daughter, she rushed in her direction leaving Monty behind. A nurse was seated beside the bed. Sarah was asleep, looking peaceful; Clarissa had to acknowledge that Sarah was peaceful only when she slept. Otherwise, her beauty was overridden by her impatience, her greed and her narcissism.

Clarissa noted that Sarah was being cared for. Her delicate pale blue gown was fresh, her hair was clean and coiffed in a soft lovely style. Her skin, though not a sick pale, was pallid from lack of sun. Monty stood beside Clarissa studying his wife revealing what she thought to be a deep longing.

A man entered the room.

"Oh," the man uttered. "Pardon me, Sir. I wasn't aware..."

"Give us a few minutes," Monty instructed turning to him. He left the room.

"What's wrong with her?" Clarissa asked, feeling Sarah's forehead. "There's no fever."

"The diagnosis is undetermined at this time," Monty answered. "Her symptoms began after we received a visit from foreigners. They may have brought with them an unknown ailment."

Monty took a step back from the bed.

"Perhaps you could visit tomorrow when she is awake," Monty suggested as he took another step.

"I thought I might stay," Clarissa responded.

"Visit tomorrow," Monty repeated turning toward the door.

Clarissa felt she had no choice but to follow and Monty called for one of his carriages to take her back to Edna's.

Meanwhile, Riley had ventured to the wharf and, finding no entertainment available, sat on a bench watching ships, row boats, wagons and carriages. It seemed to him this bustling economy could support a casino and, wondering greatly why one had not been established, his first thought was church which usually prohibited these things. Bored with sitting, he walked up the hill that led to Jesse's house and met the carriage carrying Clarissa.

"Riley!", Clarissa exclaimed, looking out the window.

"Hold up, Driver," Riley called and the carriage stopped.

Riley sat opposite his mother inside the carriage as it bolted to a start.

"You visited Sarah?" Riley asked. "How is she?"

"I'm not sure," Clarissa began thoughtfully. "She was sleeping but she looked well. There was no fever. Doctors don't know what is wrong."

The carriage took them to Edna's and she was out, walking with Becky. Riley and Clarissa sat on the porch.

"Didn't we live here once?" Riley asked.

"You were four and Sarah was two," Clarissa answered nodding. "We left when the community was struck with influenza, but your father was eager to leave anyway. The influenza became a good catapult, so to speak."

Clarissa chuckled.

"It catapulted him into his current position, actually," Clarissa added. "His knowledge of that shipping industry and that area made him a valuable asset."

"He was always lucky," Riley scoffed.

"Not luck, Son," Clarissa corrected.

"I know," Riley retorted leaning back and looking to Heaven. "God."

"I marvel that you cannot believe," Clarissa stated.

"I'd believe in God if I could see him," Riley assured her.

"Would you?" Clarissa challenged. "For Some, not believing is rejecting. And they reject so they can hold on to their sins."

"So you don't think God would want a casino built here?" Riley teased.

The next morning, Clarissa waited for the hired carriage to pick her up and, to her delight, Riley joined her stating he would go stir-crazy if he stayed behind. As before, Clarissa had her overnight bag and they were escorted into a parlor. It was a while before a young woman, who was not a servant, greeted them. This woman looking barely twenty years old was in a French empire-style dress of pale yellow chiffon. Riley cleared his throat to stifle a gasp when she appeared.

"My father is engaged," she stated with a soft voice. "I'm afraid he cannot visit with you today."

"I want to see Sarah," Clarissa stated, with slight irritation spurred by concern.

"She is quite well," declared the young woman although her brow wrinkled and she clasped her hands so that her knuckles went white. "You can visit tomorrow."

"I'm Riley," he said stepping toward her with a slight bow. "Your name?"

"Marcia," she answered, taking a step back and looking toward the door. "Please, you can visit tomorrow."

Marcia turned her back on them and went out the door. Riley took a step forward then turned toward his mother to ask, with a whisper, where Sarah was. He then continued to follow Marcia and, as they got close to the door, Riley bounded up the grand staircase to find Sarah's room.

Sarah was not in her bed and no-one was around. Returning to the hall, he followed it until he heard voices. He opened the door to a large room to see Sarah in a tub, asleep, being bathed by two women under Monty's watchful eye. Two men were standing behind Monty along with an artist holding a sketch pad. Riley's arms were then pulled from behind with such force it felt like his shoulder was being ripped off his body; he was then pushed to the ground. Though kicking and cursing, his legs were tightly bound by two other men and he was thrown into the carriage. Clarissa cried out in alarm. The carriage bolted to a start with horses racing away from the manor. When they arrived at Edna's, a man pulled Riley out of the carriage and threw him onto the yard. As he moaned in pain, Clarissa kneeled to undo the ropes. Riley told her to get a knife.

"We must tell the police," Clarissa wailed as she cut the ropes.

"This is beyond the police," Riley stated. "This man is powerful, Mother, and he knows it. He is above the law. I've met his kind many times…many times."

Edna rushed out of the house and walked with them back to the porch.

"Who told you Sarah was ill?" Riley asked Edna.

"The servants," Edna answered. "When Becky turned five, I took her to see Sarah."

"When did you see Sarah last?" Riley pressed.

"On her wedding day," Edna responded.

"This was not unusual to you?" Riley challenged.

"Are we not talking about Sarah, Riley?" Edna retorted. "Self-absorbed Sarah."

An involuntary laugh escaped from Riley and he agreed with an apology. Clarissa was staring with alarm at Riley.

"It would take an army to rescue her, Mother," Riley stated to answer her silent plea. "If she indeed wants to be rescued. That should not be assumed."

"We are not leaving until I talk to her," Clarissa insisted.

Riley moaned.

Chapter 2

Clarissa and Riley tried again to visit Sarah and, this time, they were not allowed into the building. Two men appeared: One of them holding onto the carriage horse's bridle and shouting at the carriage driver to hold up. The other man escorting them back to the carriage. As Clarissa and Riley were quiet on the way home, Riley assessed his situation. He had no money so he was not able to go anywhere to find entertainment. And, even if he made it to some entertainment, he needed money to be entertained not to mention being fed and otherwise maintained. In Edna's home he was being fed and provided comfortable accommodations. His conclusion was to try to speak to Sarah or die of boredom.

On Sunday, to Clarissa's shock, Riley accompanied her to church, not because he had seen the 'light' but because he wanted to make connections with the men in the community. He was certain entertainment was available somewhere but it was not public. It was either secret or exclusive. Not perceiving a strong church presence, he assumed it was exclusive.

At church, making sure he sat on the aisle toward the back of the sanctuary, Riley nodded with a smile to anyone who looked his way. When the service was over, he waited patiently as Clarissa talked to couples, paying attention to anything that might provide clues. He noticed a pretty young woman with almond-shaped eyes and dark brown hair walking out alone and, being a single man, wondered if she was married. To his delight, she did not get into a carriage.

"You seem to be walking my way, Miss," Riley lied with a smile.

"My husband would not want you walking with me," she responded firmly with a grim face.

"I don't see your husband," Riley quipped looking around. "How will he know?"

"He could be home when I get home," she stated then sighed. "He is here when he arrives and is gone when he leaves."

"A riddle, Ma'am?" Riley asked perplexed.

"It is a riddle that he cannot share his plans with me," she explained, talking to herself, perhaps. "Or his whereabouts or his acquaintances."

She stopped walking.

"My house is there," using her head to identify it. "Like I said, he might be in there. Good day, Sir."

Though Riley didn't want to stop, he respected her wishes and watched her disappear into the house.

At church the next Sunday, Riley pointed out the woman to Clarissa saying he wanted to know who she was. After service, Clarissa introduced herself and invited the young woman to Sunday dinner. She accepted and they learned her name, Kaylani, and her husband's name, Jesse. After an hour at the dinner table, the conversation was revealing nothing helpful so Riley sat on the porch with the men. Returning to the kitchen for a coffee, he heard someone crying as he passed the sitting room.

"He's not cruel," Kaylani said through her tears, "but he is often quite irritated. I want to please him but he doesn't explain to me what he wants."

Clarissa and Edna were both offering comfort.

"Now, when he comes home from sea," Kaylani continued, "he eats, bathes and leaves again. I may as well be living alone."

Feeling this might be the lead he was waiting for, Riley rushed to Jesse's. In the house, he opened drawers and boxes looking for anything that would reveal where Jesse goes when he leaves Kaylani. Walking into a shed in the backyard, opening drawers and boxes, he came upon sketches of nude figures, men and woman, some alone, some together, some engaged in sexual acts. Some of them Sarah. Some of them Marcia. Even to Riley's sinful mind, this was shocking. Then, hearing the sound of a shutting door, Riley slipped out of the shed unnoticed.

Back at Edna's, Riley asked Edna about Jesse. Edna relayed that Beth lived with Jesse before Kaylani came and that's all she knew. Asking the men, they said they had seen him getting supplies and they knew the name of his ship. Pleased with this progress, Riley headed to the wharf to watch for Jesse's ship to come in. When it did come in after several days, he carefully noted the direction of each sailor and spotted Jesse's trek up the hill. The next day, Riley arrived at the supply store when it opened. A few hours later, Jesse came in and, as Jesse waited for the clerk to fill his order, Riley approached him, pretending to be new in town.

"Good day, Sir," Riley greeted with a smile and a tilt of his hat.

Jesse nodded.

"I'm looking for lodging," Riley stated.

"Edna's rooming house," the clerk offered.

"Oh, only a rooming house?" Riley responded. "I was hoping for more. Perhaps some drink and company in my bed?"

Riley chuckled. The clerk ignored him.

"Won't find that here," Jesse grunted. "You'll have to travel a ways for that."

"The name of this establishment, Sir?" Riley pressed.

The clerk had filled the order and Jesse paid him. Jesse picked up as many packages as he could and Riley offered to pick up the rest. Jesse didn't object. Before Jesse climbed into the driver seat of his wagon, Riley asked again with feigned desperation.

"The name, Sir?"

"Not everyone is allowed in," Jesse stated. "You need money."

"How is one invited and how much?" Riley asked.

"I could invite you but you probably can't afford it," Jesse responded.

When Jesse gave Riley the amount, it did make Riley gulp with surprise.

"Surely, not every man pays that much," Riley declared. "I'm surprised a sailor has those means."

"It's not for sailors to be sure," Jesse agreed. "I got in at its start else I would not be welcome."

"There's no other way?" Riley pressed trying to present himself as a hungering fellow eroticist.

"I've seen other men get in by association," Jesse answered.

"Association?" Riley asked.

"A man I knew got in through a woman he was seeing," Jesse explained then he climbed on his wagon and left with no farewell.

Very pleased with this information, Riley returned to ask Edna how Sarah met Monty and, when Edna explained that Sarah built social connections starting with people that Edna knew, Riley then informed Clarissa that they were going to start making formal social calls.

It took several months of teas and balls before Riley found a suitable association. A widow, Pauline, Clarissa's age, but no where near Clarissa's beauty and grace, became smitten with Riley and called upon him often to be her companion. To his delight, he found himself in her carriage one evening driving down the long lane to Monty's manor. A hundred or so people were in attendance at a party where they were served a buffet meal and could dance if they wished. The widow did love to dance to Riley's chagrin. Throughout the night, Riley noticed groups of three to four men leaving the party then returning some time later. Suggesting to the widow that she might like some liquid refreshment, he managed to join the next group through a mysterious door.

The dark, narrow hallway led to a room that could be described as an art gallery with paintings like those in Jesse's shed. The groups of three to four men, following a cordoned path, were studying and discussing the paintings. Riley was listening to them more than he was looking at the paintings. His attention on them was interrupted by Marcia.

"Oh! It's you," Marcia cried quietly.

Riley smiled involuntarily at the sight of her and, at the same time, was aghast at her presence, knowing she was one of the models.

"Yes, it is I," Riley affirmed with a smile.

"How did you get in?" Marcia asked astounded.

"I have a more interesting question," Riley countered then he chose his words carefully. "How does a young woman like you stand in a room such as this with no discomfort?"

Marcia looked with wonder at the paintings surrounding her.

"It's art, is it not?" Marcia responded. "It's a study of a human activity many people engage in secretly. Here it is brought into the open, set free. You don't enjoy it?"

"I prefer the real thing," Riley chuckled. "I see no point in arousal with no outlet."

Marcia looked at him with a blank expression.

"You...have not engaged in this activity?" Riley dared to ask, very interested in her answer.

She blushed and looked away from him.

"You model for these pictures only?" he pressed.

"How do you know that?" Marcia blurted with shock, the blush on her face deepening.

Riley cursed at himself for assuming Marcia's sketches were public.

"I...know someone with sketches of you," Riley answered. "And Sarah, in fact."

Marcia's hand was covering her distraught face.

"You just now referred to all this as 'art,'" Riley reminded her. "Now you are reacting like it is more than art. Is it 'art' for others and something else for you? My mother would certainly not consider these pictures of Sarah as 'art.'"

Marcia rushed from the room and Riley returned to his widow with refreshment, apologizing for the delay and wondering if the brutes would appear again to expel him.

"You went to the art gallery," the widow, Pauline, guessed.

"Yes," Riley admitted, relieved that she knew.

"My husband went often," she continued with some sadness. "It's not a good practice, I think."

"How so?" Riley asked. "What is the harm?"

"The pictures are idealistic, are they not?" she explained. "It isn't fair to compare the idealistic to the real."

With a sigh, she continued.

"As I got older, my husband became less interested in me," she began as distress grew on her face. "He preferred the models in the pictures when he could get them."

"Are you saying that Monty offers these models as prostitutes?" Riley marveled. "Are you saying, if I were a member of this club, I could..."

"That's exactly what I'm saying," Pauline affirmed grimly.

"Why are you still attending these events?" Riley questioned, not understanding.

"I would sit home alone," Pauline answered.

Riley decided to tell Pauline about Sarah.

"They were sketching her as she slept?" Pauline gasped.

"My mother wants to know if Sarah has consented to this," Riley stated. "Do you know anyone close to Sarah?"

"Sarah preferred the men's company," Pauline answered. "I spoke to her briefly a few times. But I'm sure everyone in this household is sworn to secrecy and violation would have severe consequences. I'm thinking we need a spy."

Riley smiled, liking Pauline's way of thinking.

Chapter 3

A few weeks after the party, Pauline met with Riley at Edna's house; Riley wanted Pauline to meet Clarissa.

"One of my servants has a relative who has volunteered to enter into Monty's employ," Pauline announced. "She is a zealous Christian outraged at Sarah's circumstances."

"Praise God," Clarissa exclaimed. "Please express my greatest appreciation to her. I would love to meet her."

"Yes, let's arrange a meeting some time," Pauline agreed. "Let us join together to rise against this evil."

"Evil!" Riley laughed. "A bit extreme, isn't it?"

"Anything God is against is evil, Son," Clarissa answered. "You know well that God is against sex in public."

"Fortunately, that is a vice I don't have to fight," Riley stated.

"Neither does he want sex without marriage," Clarissa responded.

"Touché," Riley exclaimed.

"Neither does he want you to gamble," Clarissa added.

"I missed that commandment, Mother," Riley retorted with irritation.

"Gambling is the love of money, yes?" Clarissa reasoned. "The love of money is..."

"The root of all evil[7], right," Riley conceded.

"The rest of that verse declares that coveting money brings with it many sorrows," Clarissa stated. "Haven't you experienced many sorrows?"

Not wanting to admit it out loud, Riley had to agree, remembering the last beating he received.

Riley continued to escort Pauline as they waited for word from their spy and, as they became good friends, he found himself enjoying her company. There was a time when he would have taken Pauline to bed but, his mother's admonition about sex outside of marriage, became an obstacle. Apparently, it was an obstacle for Pauline also as she never suggested or encouraged any advances from him.

After a few months, they met with Heather, the zealous Christian spy. She said that Sarah woke up every day feeling sick, and doctors, under Monty's employ, were perpetuating this notion. After eating breakfast, doctors insisted that she exercise. They were telling her the physical therapy would make her well when in fact its purpose was to maintain her figure. When lunch was served, Monty would join her and she would launch into him with complaints and demands. He let her rant knowing that sedatives had been put in her food and she would soon sleep again. When she dozed off, he would bring in his staff to bathe and coif her then sketch her, not only in the tub but in various ways, sometimes alone, sometimes with other models, sometimes performing sexual acts including intercourse. On occasion, Monty, with his staff present, would engage himself with his sleeping wife.

This disclosure was a painful shock to everyone, including Riley and especially Clarissa. When Riley asked about Marcia, Heather reported that she rarely saw Marcia. In addition, Heather said she would not be returning to Monty's manor because she was being pressured to participate in these sessions.

Clarissa received a letter from Gordon expressing concern about her length of stay. Clarissa responded with an attempt to explain the circumstances in language appropriate for writing. She was desperate to talk with Gordon and feel his loving arms around her, shielding her from this evil. She had to admit, though, that this trial was strengthening her dependence on God[8], which is what trials are supposed to do.

Riley, finding himself concerned about Marcia, searched for a way to contact her and came to the conclusion that he would have to break into the manor. He wanted to show her the sketches of herself and

Sarah which meant he also had to break into Jesse's shed. On a Sunday, when he knew Kaylani was with Clarissa, he walked to Jesse's house. Thinking no one was home, he found the sketches in the box and turned to leave. Jesse was waiting for him.

"I'll have those," Jesse said in a threatening tone.

Riley, aware he was facing a man of strength and probably cunning, decided to appeal to any conscience he might have.

"I don't want to keep them," Riley began. "One of the ladies is my sister. The other is..."

"Marcia," Jesse interrupted. "Yes, I've known Marcia since she was born."

"You have no desire to help her?" Riley asked.

"I am helping her with those pictures hidden," Jesse revealed. "I buy up any that I see on the market. Your sister's picture was part of a packet but I recognized her as Jesse's wife."

"So do you not partake of the services offered by Monty?" Riley ventured to ask.

"I have a wife, Sir!" Jesse declared indignantly. "I would not dishonor her with that behavior."

This was not matching Kaylani's complaints but he would pursue that conflict in another conversation.

"I am quite embarrassed," Riley laughed although Jesse did not join him. "After you told me of Monty's place, I assumed...well, I got in anyway."

"Did you?" Jesse replied now showing a little amazement. "How?"

"The widow Pauline." Riley answered. "Do you know her?"

"I knew her and her husband when they were young," Jesse responded.

Jesse explained that Monty's father collected art and he sent Monty as a young man to other countries looking for additions. Jesse and Monty became friends on the sea voyages, and this is how Monty, being young and wealthy, became addicted to nudity sold as art. When

Monty began transferring his love of nudity and sex to real people, Jesse parted company. Then Jesse changed the subject.

"You're inquiries that day in the supply office were not for yourself, am I right?" Jesse guessed.

"Correct," Riley affirmed. "My mother wants to speak to Sarah and, now, I want to speak to Marcia. Marcia is not aware these sketches are public."

"You met Marcia?" Jesse questioned with suspicion.

"Yes, in the gallery. She was greeting guests," Riley answered.

"And, you want to help both of them, your sister and Marcia?" Jesse questioned again.

"Yes," Riley confirmed, "both of them."

Jesse then left as quietly as he appeared, leaving the sketches with Riley.

Heather was the next person that Riley wanted to speak to but she could not be located. Heather's parents thought she was with Edna. Pauline's servants had no knowledge of her whereabouts. Riley began to fear that Heather had been abducted and returned to Monty's manor. Realizing that Heather had placed herself in danger to help Sarah, Riley decided to do the same. After hiking for several hours, Riley arrived at the lane to the manor and he followed it to the stone wall surrounding the property. Climbing a tree, he saw the guards who had removed him once before and some dogs. Watching them for a while, he saw them walking in a pattern that might allow him to get into the house. As the sun began to set, he was delighted to see Marcia come out of a door and follow a path around the garden. He observed, if she followed the path, she would go to the far end of the property and arrive at a tree that was climbable. Sprinting around the stone wall to the tree, he quickly climbed it and saw her approach.

"Marcia," Riley said softly so as not to alarm the dogs.

Marcia stopped and looked around. Not seeing Riley, she continued her walk.

"Marcia, over here," Riley said again and this time Marcia moved in his direction.

"Oh, it's you!" she exclaimed.

"Yes, here I am again," Riley said with a smile, tipping his hat best he could.

"Why are you up there?" Marcia asked innocently.

"Don't you know your father threw me out?" Riley asked with wonder. "And he won't let me back in."

"Yes, but you invaded a private area," Marcia answered flatly. "He meant no harm."

"He meant no harm?" Riley scoffed remembering the pain of that encounter. "Let me assure you his actions were harmful."

"Come down from there," Marcia commanded as she giggled at him.

"Am I safe from the guards and the dogs?" Riley asked surveying the garden. "Are you sure?"

"They will come if I call for them," Marcia replied. "It's up to you, I guess, if I call for them or not."

Riley jumped down bringing leaves with him. Brushing himself off he then followed Marcia to a bench.

Marcia looked at him with innocent eyes waiting for him to speak.

"I have the sketches," Riley declared pulling them out of his backpack.

He offered them to her and she reached for them slowly, with dread, then gasped as they came into her view.

"These were not to be circulated," Marcia stated, mostly to herself. "These were the last..."

"The last..." Riley encouraged as she trailed off.

Marcia explained that she was raised to be comfortable with nudity. She was taught that being nude was being free and regular sketches were made of her as she grew up.

"Why was this the last one?" Riley pressed.

"Something in me wanted to stop," Marcia answered. "I can't explain it. I couldn't explain it to my father but he respected my wishes. I'm certain he would not have offered these for sale."

Riley knew in himself that 'something' was Marcia's conscience. It was the same 'something' that he wrestled with on a daily basis as he pursued opportunities to gamble.

"Do you know Edna's rooming house?" Riley asked. "That's where I live with my mother, Clarissa. I want you to come to Sunday dinner. Can you do that? At 1 PM?"

Marcia studied Riley's face and nodded as though mesmerized.

Riley woke early on Sunday surprising Clarissa with his smiling presence at breakfast. This was so unlike the Riley who took no interest in any day at Edna's that did not advance him toward his beloved casinos. Though he did not attend church, he chatted with Edna as she cooked with Becky at her side. He even helped set the table, looking at his watch more than usual. Around 12:30 Clarissa returned with Kaylani, both offering to help Edna. Riley escaped the overcrowded kitchen to sit on the porch with the men, studying every carriage as it went by. Close to 1 PM, Edna announced that dinner was ready and the men left the porch. Riley lingered, starting to get disappointed. He could hear the tapping of silverware on plates as people ate and talked. Stepping off the porch to survey the street, he gave up and headed to the dining room when he heard talking outside. Turning quickly, he rushed with delight to greet Marcia, who was being helped out of the carriage. She apologized for being late, a little flustered, and didn't seem to notice that Riley had his hand on the small of her back as they walked toward the house. Putting his hand there was not a deliberate move; it sort of went there on its own, naturally.

Marcia stayed quiet at the table but she was observant, smiling and laughing sometimes. Becky gave her a lot of attention and Riley wondered if this was because Marcia was pretty and dressed beautifully. This was his first good look at her actually and he loved having the opportunity. Porcelain smooth skin surrounded her light blue eyes, delicate nose and lips. Ringlets of light brown hair escaped the ornament that pulled the rest of her hair away from her face. Marcia gave Becky her full attention and, if Marcia did speak, her words and gestures were graceful. He found himself upset that any other man may have seen those sketches and was grateful to Jesse for hiding them.

In the sitting room, Kaylani again talked about her distress over Jesse, and Marcia listened with interest then joined the conversation.

"Wasn't he married before?" Marcia asked. "I thought he was married."

"Beth lived there..." Edna started to say.

"Not his wife!" Kaylani cried with tears. "A hoar! I thought she was a housekeeper but she was his hoar!"

Her outburst stunned the room. Clarissa rose and asked Riley to leave; she shut the door to the sitting room. When the ladies emerged some time later, Kaylani, though not happy, was at least smiling politely. Marcia and Clarissa embraced before Marcia walked to the door. Riley accompanied her, bursting with curiosity, and he invited her to come back. He nearly tripped dashing to his mother.

"What happened?" Riley blurted to Clarissa.

"Well, it seems, after Beth left, Jesse said her name in his sleep," Clarissa stated with some uncharacteristic irritation. "When Kaylani asked him about it, he gave no explanation. Her reaction to that was to spurn his advances which led him to abandon her, I guess, one would call it."

"Actually, I spoke to him and he's not going to Monty's," Riley mused. "I wonder where he goes."

"We prayed about it," Clarissa added. "God will help if he can."

"If he can? I thought he could do all things," Riley challenged.

"He doesn't violate your will, Riley," Clarissa responded. "At the same time, you have two choices: Heaven or Hell. I would choose Heaven, if I were you."

"Church or a casino, Mother?" Riley whined. "There is no comparison."

"The Body of Christ or a casino, Riley," Clarissa retorted. "The creator of the universe or a casino, Riley. Before you choose the casino, you should research the alternative."

Ignoring his mother, Riley made up his mind to find out where Jesse was going. Then he wanted to extract Marcia away from her father and find a way to talk to Sarah. Before he was able to begin those tasks, he heard from Pauline that Heather's body was delivered to her family in a heap, beaten to death.

Chapter 4

The casket at Heather's funeral was closed. The congregation, heartbroken, was solemn as the minister reviewed Heather's short, Jesus-filled life. Riley didn't hear the minister's words because his heart was pierced with the fact that Heather sacrificed herself for his sister. A picture was lodged in his brain of himself at the gambling table while Heather was tortured. In his sleep that night, it became his nightmare. To his horror, the vision of Heather morphed into thousands and thousands of sinners, including Marcia, falling into the burning lake of fire[9]. Finally, crying out, his mother rushed to his side and, hearing his description of the dream, she urged him to cry out to Jesus.

The next morning, inspired by Heather's courage, Riley knocked on Jesse's door and was relieved when he answered.

"Walk with me, will you?" Riley asked and Jesse complied. "I gave the sketches to Marcia but I didn't tell her you had them."

Jesse grunted his acknowledgement.

"My mother attends church with Kaylani," Riley began. "Did you know?"

"She told me," Jesse confirmed.

"Women talk," Riley laughed to indicate a feigned disdain for that behavior, "and I happened to overhear."

Riley could see, in spite of his sour demeanor, Jesse was interested.

"Are you spending a lot of time away from her?" Riley asked with all his courage.

"That's why you asked if I was going to Monty's," Jesse concluded then sighed deeply. "For my reputation's sake I will tell you, I took a job about 20 miles from here."

He stopped walking and looked down at his boots.

"She seemed to need the space," Jesse added.

"She needs to know you want her," Riley stated bravely.

"Why isn't that obvious!" Jesse blurted. "I married her! What more can I say to the woman?"

His anger released a torrent of words that had probably built up since Beth left.

"I intended to marry Beth," he grumbled, mostly to himself, again looking at his boots, "but she gave herself to me without marriage. As time went by, it seemed like an unnecessary formality. Then, when I met Kaylani and she was responsive to me, I admit, I let my eyes and my physical desire override my head. Beth was…"

"Beth doesn't belong to you now," Riley found himself saying. "You proposed to Kaylani and she accepted, believing in you. Fulfilling that commitment is your responsibility and at this time, your partnership is failing. You're in a storm, Brother; you know what to do in a storm."

Riley's hand landed on Jesse's shoulder and to his amazement, Jesse returned the gesture. Their eyes met then Jesse turned back to his house. Amazed at this encounter, Riley decided the advice he shared with Jesse must have come from his father in a lecture long ago. Feeling confident, he moved to his next task, talking to Sarah.

When he returned to Edna's, he was greeted with joy by his father, Gordon. Clarissa was beside herself with excitement. Going to the sitting room to catch up, Gordon said he had been stressing over the distance between himself and his family not to mention the threats he was receiving to pay Riley's debts. But, the news of Heather's death was the final straw. With Beth and Jonathan's help, Gordon had everything moved to their farm and he sold the house. Beth and Jonathan welcomed Lorilai, Tyler's child, into their home, thanking God for the privilege. Asked about his plans, Gordon said they would find a house and a job then he would let God lead and guide him. With a deep sigh and a shift, Riley expressed frustration that Gordon recognized.

"Give God a chance, Riley," Gordon urged. "Let's get out of his way and give him a chance."

"Heather is dead!" Riley blurted. "Is Sarah next? Is Marcia next?"

"God had his reasons for taking Heather," Gordon insisted. "It's not our place to know or question."

Seeing that his son was not being comforted, he rose and took his wife outside for a walk. Watching them walk towards the woods, Riley pictured himself walking with Marcia as his wife.

The next day, Gordon was waiting for Riley to come down for breakfast; Gordon wanted to visit Heather's minister. On borrowed horses, they had to travel a few hours to arrive at the parish. The minister, Edward Simmons and his wife, Abigail, welcomed them graciously and offered lunch where they asked each other 'get-acquainted' questions. Going to Edward's study, Gordon asked about Heather.

"A tragic loss for the world," Edward started, "a wondrous gain for our Savior's Kingdom in Heaven. Heather was blessed at an early age with knowledge of who Jesus was and what he did for us. Sometimes the Holy Spirit touches people with that gift of faith, you know?"

"Yes," Gordon agreed. "I've met a few like that. Nothing can shake them. But, has her death been investigated by authorities?"

"No authority like that is established here," Edward answered, "and the crime wasn't committed here. I've lived here my whole life. People here follow Jesus and those that don't want to follow him, move away."

"I see," Gordon responded with a nod of approval. "Jesus is the authority in this community."

Gordon and Travis next went to the police station on the wharf and it was no surprise that they were unaware of Heather's death. The police chief did express concern and offered assistance.

When they returned to Edna's, Riley asked for the next move.

"You won't understand this, Son," Gordon stated. "I'm starting a Bible study."

"You got that right!" Riley blurted laughing. "How will that help!"

"Edward gave us the answer," Gordon explained. "Communities that follow Jesus live in peace. People who follow Jesus don't kill and, by the way, they don't fornicate."

"Or gamble," Riley added.

"Right," Gordon agreed. "God is superior to any casino, Riley. God can match and exceed whatever pleasure you derive from gambling...or any sin for that matter."

In the coming month, Gordon and Clarissa found a house and started a Bible study. Edna, Becky and two of Edna's tenants attended. Kaylani eventually joined. Seeing that no-one owned their own Bible, Gordon ordered a crate of Bibles from the supply store. When they arrived, Gordon handed them out to anyone who would take them. The police chief and the supply store owner let Gordon hang a notice advertising the Bible study held at his home on Wednesday nights. To Riley's amazement, the next time Kaylani arrived at Gordon's house, Jesse was with her. Kaylani's countenance was changed completely from a grim, unhappy woman to a content wife. Jesse sat close to her with his arm on the back of her chair and he smiled at her sometimes in response to something she said to him. To everyone's delight, Kaylani announced that their baby was expected later that year. Marcia came immediately to Riley's mind and he wondered what the possibilities were of Marcia carrying his child.

When Gordon was done with that night's teaching, and the group enjoyed refreshments, Jesse asked Gordon and Riley about Sarah and Marcia. Gordon relayed their recent visit to Sarah and Riley relayed everything he knew including Heather's report that Sarah was being put to sleep every day. Jesse, noting that Sarah would be awake for lunch, suggested that the three of them visit at that time. When Riley relayed that guards had thrown him out by force, Jesse proposed that they find volunteers to go with them. Gordon believed the police chief would go and the two tenants said they would help.

The next day, the six men waited in the parlor for Monty. When a servant said Monty wasn't available, the group, led by Jesse, walked up the grand staircase and into Sarah's room.

"Father?" Sarah exclaimed as Monty turned with shock.

Responding to a signal given by Monty, a man left the room. Monty noticed Jesse but turned to his wife.

"Sarah!" Gordon blurted as he rushed to her side.

"Guards are coming!" Riley cried and handed the sketches to Sarah.

Sarah lifted one of the sketches and gazed at it. Jesse and the three other men formed a line to receive the guards.

"Is that me?" Sarah whispered with awe as she touched the sketch gently. "I'm so beautiful!"

Her face turned to question Monty who was gazing at her intently.

"You are beautiful, My Darling," Monty answered.

Sarah picked up another sketch.

"Who is this?" Sarah whispered again with awe, touching a nude man in the picture.

"Manuel," Monty answered softly, amazed at Sarah's reaction.

The guards entered the room.

"Hold!" Monty commanded, not removing his eyes from his wife.

"You're letting him do that to me?" Sarah asked in a low voice, leaning close to Monty. She was smiling impishly.

Monty shifted as his body responded with arousal.

"Would you let him do that to me if I was awake?" she asked as innocently as a child asking for ice cream.

"To create art, yes I would," Monty replied but quickly added. "First and foremost, you are my wife. Doing that to you is my privilege."

"But to create art..." Sarah repeated then she picked up another sketch and gasped. "This too?"

"Sarah!" Gordon exclaimed, distressed at what he was witnessing. "God is against this!"

"Silence, Sir!" Monty commanded. "Or you will be removed!"

Gordon dropped to his knees and began pleading, with tears, to God to have mercy on his daughter.

"Sarah, I must explain," Monty went on. "You are difficult when you are awake, don't you know? You are impossible! No-one can live with you!"

"He's right, Sarah," Riley offered. "If I had to live with you, I also would put you to sleep."

"Riley," Gordon, in his angst, begged. "We must pray for Sarah! We must pray!"

"I'm not sick?" Sarah mused and went back to the picture of Manuel. "If I behave, we can create art with Manuel?"

As Sarah waited with anticipation for her husband's answer, Monty, overcome with passion, leaned forward and caressed his wife's lips as his hand gently massaged her breast. Gordon rose abruptly and rushed away from them pulling Riley along. Jesse and the others followed him. In the carriage, seeing Gordon's distress, Jesse offered solace.

"She made her choice," Jesse stated.

"She got what she always wanted," Riley mocked. "The Princess is on her throne."

"She's damned to Hell," Gordon exclaimed, his face wet with tears, looking to Heaven. "She's turned her back on God and she's damned to Hell."

Riley then remembered his nightmare with some discomfort.

Chapter 5

With Sarah's case closed, Riley turned his attention to Marcia and sent her an invitation to another Sunday dinner. To his great delight, she accepted; he marveled that his excitement to see her exceeded any past excitement for any event. As he did before, he sat with the men on the porch waiting for her carriage and rushed to her when it appeared. Once again, during dinner, Becky lavished attention on her and Marcia graciously responded. She helped Kaylani, Edna and Clarissa clear the table and stayed in the kitchen. The women talked of recipes, housekeeping, fashion, Kaylani's baby then they went into the sitting room with Becky, not inviting Riley to join. Gordon was on the porch talking with the men.

Riley sat down on the steps of the staircase to wait for Marcia. Women, in Riley's past social experience, were always available to him, many seeking his attention. And those who did not seek his attention, were easily accessed with a few charming words. For him to want a woman's attention so badly and have it denied him was perplexing. He almost felt like praying for help.

Marcia emerged from the room with Kaylani and, seeing Riley on the steps, said his name. Riley scrambled to his feet surprised to see Marcia carrying a Bible. Announcing that she had to leave, he walked her to the porch. She stopped to speak to Gordon who rose, along with the other men.

"I hope to see you on Wednesday," Marcia said to Gordon.

"It is my hope as well," Gordon responded.

Marcia said farewell to Riley as he helped her into the coach and she was gone. It felt like a light in Riley's soul was turned off.

After the Bible study on the following Wednesday, Marcia stayed behind in the sitting room as Clarissa and Gordon ushered their guests out of the house. Though Riley was with her, she didn't speak to him; lost in her own thoughts. Seeming to know that Marcia was waiting for them, Clarissa and Gordon returned asking if she would like refreshments. When she declined, they sat with her. She opened her Bible and read:

"First Corinthians, chapter 6, verses 9 and 10. The Apostle Paul is speaking, I believe:

'Do you not know that the unrighteous will not inherit the kingdom of God? Do not be deceived. Neither fornicators, nor idolaters, nor adulterers, nor homosexuals, ...will inherit the kingdom of God.[10],

If a fornicator is one who admires nudity as art, then, according to this verse, my father and I will not inherit the kingdom of God. What does that mean exactly?"

"When we choose to follow Jesus," Gordon explained, "he becomes our king and we become his subjects in this world and also in Heaven. Jesus does not authorize any of the behaviors in that verse therefore, those following him will not practice them."

"I see," Marcia nodded.

"Since you found this verse, I must assume you read the entire Bible," Gordon guessed.

"Yes," Marcia answered.

"You saw then references to the alternative?" Gordon pressed.

"The burning lake of fire[11], yes," Marcia answered with a wrinkle in her brow.

"It should be an easy decision, don't you think?" Gordon challenged.

"One would think," Marcia responded. "I am amazed how hard the decision is. I would have to leave my father. Even if I had a place to go..."

"You can stay at Edna's," Riley inserted with excitement.

"You can stay here," Clarissa quickly corrected.

"Even with your kind invitation, I'm expecting my father to be upset," Marcia explained. "He doesn't agree with Christianity and would consider me lost to a cult. I would be giving up everything I have ever known."

"And gaining everything you ever wanted," Gordon added urgently. "Gaining more than you wanted, in fact. Or gaining something you didn't know you wanted."

Marcia rose stating she needed to get back. Gordon invited her to church and Sunday dinner. Riley escorted her to the carriage wanting so much to talk to her but she was lost in her own thoughts and he didn't disturb her.

On Sunday morning, Riley was ready for church and waiting for Marcia's carriage which didn't arrive. Neither did it arrive at 1 PM. Stopping his father before he sat down to dinner, Riley expressed concern about Marcia's absence. Though Gordon tried to assure him that everything was probably alright, Riley continued to be concerned. Wondering if Jesse could help, Kaylani reported that Jesse wasn't home. Riley grabbed his backpack and headed to Marcia's on foot.

Climbing the same tree, he saw the guards and dogs as before but Marcia didn't come out to walk like she did before. As it got dark, he saw again the guard's pattern and calculated when he would make an attempt to enter the building. As the opening occurred, he managed to lower himself onto the ground safely then he sprinted to the door where Marcia had emerged before. It led to a dark, quiet hallway and opened into a kitchen, now vacant. Two doors led out of the kitchen. Riley's sense of direction told him that the door on his right led to the back of the house and the door in front of him would lead to the grand staircase.

Opening the door slowly and turning right, he entered a large hall. Turning back to the left, he climbed the grand staircase. Knowing the location of Sarah's room, Riley turned the opposite direction and came to a locked door. Hearing a noise, he slipped behind a curtain and when no-one approached him, he crept closer toward Sarah's room keeping his head down. Marcia was being escorted down the hall with a guard and was let into a room. To Riley's horror, the guard locked the door. Deciding there was nothing further he could do by himself, he rushed down the grand staircase and headed for the front door. Nearly reaching it, he was tackled and bludgeoned.

Riley woke up, naked, in a comfortable bed with a canopy in a beautifully furnished room; walls covered with Monty's art. On the bed-stand was a sketch of his nude body lying peacefully in the bed. He ripped it to shreds. The door was locked, of course, as was the window. Hearing footsteps in the hall, he knocked on the door and a guard pushed it open telling Riley he would return shortly. "Shortly" was quite a while but he returned with a tray of food then he left. Riley was enjoying the food when Monty entered with a guard.

"Is everything to your liking?" Monty asked as he drew a chair across from Riley.

"My compliments to your chef," Riley quipped.

"I could have disposed of you," Monty began casually.

"Like Heather?" Riley interrupted.

"That didn't have to happen," Monty stated with irritation. "I am not a fan of violence and I am a fair man. But she made the mistake of trying to evangelize her very first client and she reaped the consequences. In your case, this can be ended peacefully if you board a ship and never return. I will pay your passage."

"Not gonna happen, My Friend," Riley answered. "I find myself wanting to take Marcia as my wife."

"Yes, that's obvious," Monty muttered with a sigh. "You do have some other choices other than disposal. You can stay here, be a model and entertain my guests."

"A prostitute?" Riley mused.

"To begin with," Monty began, "and, as you become trusted, you would be given clothes and allowed to socialize. Many here live in luxury they would never know elsewhere."

"I prefer freedom," Riley responded. "How many prostitutes work here?"

"Sex slave then," Monty continued ignoring Riley's question. "Assuming you would not cooperate, I have many clients who like a feisty encounter. I would leave myself the option to sell or trade you."

"Your attempt to scare me isn't working," Riley stated. "You know my family will look for me if I don't return home. They may be on there way here as we speak."

"They have already inquired, in fact," Monty replied, "and I agree with you. They will be back, probably with Jesse and the police like they did before."

Monty reached his hand to the guard who handed him sketches. Riley fell back in his chair at the drawings of Marcia engaged in sexual acts.

"Those sketches aren't based on real life," Monty stated. "She has withdrawn her consent to be a model and shows no interest in sexual activity. She is, however, under my complete control. Many clients want her virginity and will pay handsomely whether she relinquishes it voluntarily or under force. I promise you this will happen. If you love her, as you say you do, take my offer to board a ship and never return."

Monty rose from the chair, leaving the sketches with Riley that he ripped to pieces. The guard took the tray of food. Riley remained slumped in the chair paralyzed with helplessness. His mind was telling him to board the ship. His love for Marcia was demanding her rescue. With his mind protesting the decision, arguing that God would not listen to a sinner like him, he knelt.

"My Heavenly Father," Riley began, reciting what he had heard many times, "will you help me? Will you help Marcia? It seems only fair to offer you something in return and I offer to turn from gambling and follow Jesus. I'll be honest with you, I offer to turn from gambling to gain Marcia. But I pray for the day that I can say honestly that I love you and honor you as much as my parents do."

A warm feeling overcame Riley he had never experienced before as sobs broke through from the depth of his soul. As he wept, a door opened. The guard had returned and started disrobing. Riley watched with amazement aware that the man was there to rape. With his clothes off, the man took two steps to Riley putting his stinking groin in Riley's face. Looking up at the man with a smile, Riley caressed the man's crotch until he was fully aroused and the man was shutting his eyes in ecstasy, moaning. Urging him to lay down on the floor, promising something special, the man complied. When the man started begging for his swollen organ to be inserted somewhere, Riley squeezed and twisted it with all his strength. As the man crumpled in pain, Riley punched it ferociously a few more times. Walking over to a chest of drawers, he tipped it so that it fell on the man and he cried out. Assuming the man's cry was heard, Riley grabbed the man's shirt and left the room. He was in a long hallway with several doors. Finding one unlocked, he entered and put on the shirt, a few sizes too big for him. A young woman was in the room at a vanity.

"Are you lost?" she asked looking at his reflection in the mirror.

"No, Ma'am," Riley answered and he escaped through the window.

On the roof and seeing the front entrance, he calculated where he might find Marcia. Walking as briskly as possible toward the end of the building, he was glad to see a porch roof he could reach. Hoping he was under the window to Marcia's room, he pulled himself up to look in. She was in the room but not alone. He believed his only course was to wait until nightfall and pray that Monty would not violate Marcia in the meantime. As a light appeared in Marcia's window, Riley again pulled himself up and tapped his head on the pane.

"Riley! Riley!" Marcia whispered with great distress as tears ran down her face; she opened the window and helped him get in.

He engulfed her in his arms, looking to Heaven with thanksgiving. Though he wanted to hold her forever, he stepped back.

"We must leave!" he exclaimed in a whisper.

"There is a trap door in Father's study," Marcia stated, "but my door is locked."

Riley walked to Marcia's vanity and picked up some hair pins. With one of them, he was able to pick the lock. Marcia said she wanted to see which guards were on duty. Riley watched her walk down the hall, down the grand staircase, disappearing from his sight. He closed his eyes wondering if she was betraying him. The next few minutes took forever to pass then she reappeared.

"I passed one guard in the hall going to the study," Marcia reported. "The rest must be looking for you. I can handle the dog."

Marcia led Riley to a hall with gigantic windows on one side and numerous doors on the other. Riley followed Marcia ducking behind furniture. When she approached the guard, she called his name and he went to her. She greeted the dog, petting him and took his leash offering to walk with him. Marcia was pointing outside telling the guard she heard something from her room. He informed her that an intruder was being pursued. Riley leaped on the man tumbling down with him and got on top of him, pummeling repeatedly with his fists. With curses, the man kicked, rolled and grabbed at Riley, trying to raise up.

"Marcia, kick his groin!" Riley bellowed.

"His what?" Marcia cried.

"His groin, groin," Riley repeated.

"Groin?" Marcia said as she rushed next to Riley.

Riley grabbed the dog's leash and held it to the man's throat until he passed out.

"Some day, I'm going to show you a groin!" Riley promised as he ran with Marcia to her father's study.

Dropping down the trap door into blackness, Marcia led the way and Riley had no idea what his bare feet were walking on. It didn't feel like grass. Finally Marcia stopped and opened a door built into an embankment of a river. Without stopping, she ran to a rowboat pushing it into the water. Riley grabbed the oars and maneuvered the boat in the direction Marcia indicated. They were going downstream so he only had to keep the boat away from obstacles. Marcia sat quietly across from him. He could see only her silhouette so he had no clue what she was experiencing. He was experiencing a peace he had never, ever known before. Looking to Heaven, he thanked God.

It was daybreak when Riley pounded on Gordon and Clarissa's door. Gordon answered and with a cry of relief, embraced his son. He called to Clarissa to come downstairs and bring a robe. Going into the sitting room, Riley collapsed on the biggest, most comfortable overstuffed chair available. Marcia went to the kitchen to help Clarissa get coffee. Riley studied his father who was sitting across from him.

"I'm following Jesus, Father," Riley stated quietly, knowing the words alone would overwhelm Gordon.

And they did. Gordon raised his hands to Heaven and looked up with tears escaping. Riley repeated the words when Clarissa entered and, quickly sitting down a tray of coffee, she rushed to kneel beside her son. They embraced. Riley realized his father was right when he said God is better than gambling. Riley had never experienced the joy and contentment he was experiencing now.

Marcia remained quiet as they drank coffee and Riley described, in general, what happened. When Clarissa rose to take the tray to the kitchen, Marcia went also. Then, Riley was disappointed to see Clarissa escorting Marcia upstairs.

"Is she alright?" Riley asked Clarissa when she returned.

"Physically she is alright," Clarissa answered. "But, she has lost everything she has ever known. You have been in that position, have you not?"

"Yes," Riley agreed thoughtfully, with an understanding he didn't have before. "She gave up everything. Another sacrifice...like Heather."

The three of them sat quietly for a few moments.

"I want to marry Marcia," Riley announced. "I need to talk to her."

Both parents shifted uncomfortably. Gordon cleared his throat.

"Are you planning to work?" Gordon asked.

"Yes, Sir," Riley answered humbly. "Wherever I can."

"I can speak to her for you," Gordon offered, "and we can begin the courting process."

"A little old-fashioned, don't you think?" Riley whined.

"God doesn't think so, I assure you," Clarissa retorted. "You both must be protected from your passions."

Gordon rose from his seat, grabbed a Bible and handed it to his son, suggesting that he learn it.

Chapter 6

The next day, Marcia came to the breakfast table saying that she had to return to her father's house. When Gordon and Clarissa ask why, she said that her father would come for her and she feared what he would do. They urged her to wait until they could get Riley.

"If you go back," Riley exclaimed, "I'm going with you."

"Father will kill you!" Marcia cried.

"He might," Riley responded glibly, "Or he might let me work for him. If I gain his trust, I'll be able to socialize and I'll be close to you."

"Hold on!" Gordon interrupted. "Both of you need to stay here. The police here will offer as much protection as they are able."

Riley scoffed.

"And we will pray," Gordon added.

With Marcia and Riley promising to stay, the four of them prayed for God's guidance and protection. Gordon and Riley met with the police chief to share their fear of Monty's retribution. Marcia started helping Edna with housekeeping and cooking and Riley went to work at the supply store. With Gordon, Clarissa or Edna as a chaperone, Riley was allowed to spend time with Marcia and they talked of their future together.

Monty and Sarah soon called on Clarissa and she greeted them graciously, as though nothing had happened.

"We were hoping to see Marcia," Monty stated when Clarissa brought refreshments into the sitting room.

"She is out at the moment," Clarissa responded not wanting to share Marcia's location.

"Please tell her we called," Monty requested. "Is there a wedding date?"

"Nothing final," Clarissa replied.

"Riley works at the supply store, yes?" Monty said with some sarcasm; Sarah rolled her eyes.

"He does," Clarissa affirmed.

"It might be a while before he can afford a wife, don't you think?" Monty guessed.

"It might," Clarissa agreed.

"She would be better off with me, in the long run," Monty mused, "and a husband of means."

"Pardon me for disagreeing, Sir," Clarissa stated, looking deliberately at Sarah, "Riley will sustain her and their family with God's love and God's provision. She will prosper in ways that you do not understand."

"I am a fair man, Madam, and I will be honest," Monty stated with distress. "I want her with me and her absence is painful enough but to know she has been tricked into believing in this God myth is unbearable."

"On some level, you know God is not a myth," Clarissa began, "or at least at some point you knew. You have obviously chosen Sin as your master and God will not interfere."

"I choose truth and freedom, Madam," Monty blurted now getting agitated.

Clarissa rose.

"You might be more comfortable taking your leave, Sir," Clarissa suggested.

Monty left the room and Clarissa touched Sarah's arm.

"There is a place for you here, Sarah," Clarissa said warmly. "If you want to turn from Sin, there is a place for you here."

Sarah left with no response and no reaction.

Clarissa shared the conversation with Gordon and Riley so, assuming Monty would attempt to abduct Marcia, they hired a police officer to stay with Marcia when she was at Edna's and she was not allowed to go anywhere on her own. They feared also, that Monty could abduct Clarissa or Becky or anyone for that matter to gain leverage. They knew their only real hope was in how God chose to answer their prayers.

After a few weeks, at the supply store one day, sailors rushed into the store.

"We must evacuate to higher ground!" they cried. "The sea is receding; it's a tsunami!"

Riley ran outside amazed to see water going in reverse, leaving giant ships stranded. Then he ran to Gordon and Clarissa's to repeat the news. Both jumped to their feet. Gordon and Riley ran to neighbors and Clarissa stuffed provisions into flour sacks. Rushing upstairs, she grabbed blankets, clothes and a box of money and important papers. Neighbors with wagons lined up and people loaded them. Jesse drove up in a wagon with Kaylani and their baby boy then he loaded provisions being brought to him. People with horses were riding house to house to be sure no-one was left behind. The community left, up the hill toward Jesse's house then past the cemetery where Tyler was laid and past the land once owned by Beth and Richard. In a while they came to Monty's estate and Jesse turned down the lane then entered the building.

"You are warning my father?" Marcia asked in amazement.

"And Sarah," Clarissa added.

" '...pray for them which despitefully use you, and persecute you'[12] ?" Gordon responded to Marcia. "Remember that verse?"

Marcia, recognizing God's love flowing through Gordon and Clarissa, folded her hands in prayer, closed her eyes and began sobbing. Riley, knowing he would not have chosen to warn Monty and Sarah, asked God to, not only forgive the hate in his heart, but replace it with the kind of love his father had just exhibited.

When the community reached the highest hill available, someone shouted that the wave was coming in; most people rushed to watch. The beauty of the white-capped wave hid its power. It crushed ships and moved buildings off their foundations like they were toys. As the buildings rode the currents, they crashed into each other creating driftwood. To everyone's amazement, the water climbed the hill coming closer to them. Jesse yelled at them to get back fearing the ground beneath them would crumble. The water's progress did stop just below the hill and withdrew taking with it the rubble it had created. When the wave reached the sea, other smaller waves followed but eventually, the normal wave pattern returned.

The community set up camp and shared what they had with their neighbors. Riley and Marcia went to Gordon to tell him they wanted to be married. Gordon found the community minister and a ceremony was arranged. Edna gave Riley her wedding ring. With a blanket and a burning log from the campfire, Riley led Marcia away from the group, started a fire and, showing her his groin, physically shared it with her, as God designed.

The next morning, Jesse, Gordon, Riley and other men, looking over the hill, were no longer standing on a hill, but a cliff. The road they had driven the night before was washed away. The mature trees whose roots were once dug into the soil were laying flat below them. As they followed the ridge, they saw that Monty's manor was gone. Continuing to follow the ridge, they came to a hill they could descend which led to the sea. From there they were able to explore the area that once was their home. Jesse, Gordon and Riley broke off and headed toward the location of Monty's manor. As they got closer to the cliff and the sun reached the noon position, something on the ground started to glimmer. Jesse commented that it looked like gold but he wasn't serious. To their amazement, however, it was gold - gold ingots and figures. Looking up, Riley saw the opening of the tunnel he and Marcia had escaped through. In addition, almost directly under the tunnel opening was a large chest, locked. Riley was able to pick the lock with Jesse's knife and the chest contained jewels, 'art' of Marcia at various ages and 'art' sketches of Monty with a woman. In some of the sketches the woman was pregnant. Wanting to notify Marcia, the men covered these findings with trees and returned to camp.

The next day, on horses, with shovels and sacks, the men returned with Marcia. Riley dressed her in pants and boots and smiled at how she looked, planning to dress her like that often. Marcia marveled at the gold but was not surprised; she knew her father had a stash of gold. The chest mesmerized her. The woman was her mother who she didn't remember, but her father had shared the pictures.

"Is this enough to rebuild the community?" Marcia asked hopefully.

The men gazed at the young woman with wonder.

"You would use this wealth to build a house for me?" Jesse stammered in disbelief.

"We don't know where you father is," Gordon stated. "He could have escaped."

"That's true," Marcia agreed. "But the jewels are mine."

Gordon, overwhelmed with thanksgiving, knelt to lead the group in prayer. He asked God to bless this wealth and he prayed for it to be used to God's glory. He asked God to reward Marcia for her generosity.

Riley, studying one of the gold pieces, felt an old urge to take possession of the treasure. His thoughts were telling him he could convince Marcia to keep it and they could return to Great Britain to live in a luxurious manor like his wealthy friends. Unlike his gambling days, however, another voice was speaking reminding him of the sorrow attached to the enticing piece. He saw clearly he had a choice: Heaven or Hell. He dropped the piece into a bag with the others.

Jesse was acquainted with merchants who transported goods on his ship and he was able to get Marcia's jewels appraised. He had to sell only a couple of items to cover the cost of building materials and supplies. Under the tunnel opening, a compound of homes was built for Marcia, Riley, Gordon, Clarissa, Jesse, Kaylani and their baby, and Edna and her tenants. Interest free loans were given to other residents leading to

Gordon and Riley evolving into a real estate office. Jesse met with his ship's owners to raise funds to rebuild the wharf. He became a leader of a coalition of ship owners and merchants. Gordon and Riley worked with the community minister to build a large Christian church and social gathering place in the center of the resurrected town. Gordon held his Wednesday Bible studies there with the hope that Jesus would become the authority of the community.

When it was decided to sell more jewels, Riley and Jesse travelled to the exchange house. As they approached their destination, Riley saw a woman who looked like Sarah coming out of a building. He called her name and, when she looked up, he jumped from the wagon.

"Sarah?" Riley asked.

"Yes," she cooed. "Riley, what a surprise."

"How are you!" Riley exclaimed, truly happy to see her alive. "You look well."

"I'm alright," Sarah answered, completely uninterested in the conversation. "I'm on stage, you know."

"Are you?" Riley responded, starting to be sorry he saw her. "I'm glad to see you escaped."

"Yes, we got out through a tunnel," Sarah droned. "It was a struggle at first but Monty was able to quickly sell his art to feed us then he built his house of pleasure. We are presenting 'living art' now and it is immensely popular. You should visit; Monty often refers to Jesse's warning with gratitude. I'm sure you all would be welcome."

"Sarah," Riley began softly, taking her hand, "God is against Monty's art. When you leave this earth..."

"Spare me!" Sarah snapped, pulling her hand away and turning from him. "I've heard this a hundred times. Christians here constantly harass us."

"God will let you go, Sarah," Riley pleaded. "You will no longer be his. You will belong to the Kingdom of Darkness; to the Prince of Darkness."

"So be it," Sarah concluded and walked away.

Riley told Gordon, Clarissa and Marcia about meeting Sarah, and they decided to send Monty's gold to her.

As the years passed, God blessed them all with children and prosperity as ships and trade resumed, better than it was before. Riley often laughed at himself remembering how he had once given his life to gambling with black eyes and swollen lips as his reward. He remembered with warmth in his heart Gordon's statement:

"God is superior to any casino. God can match and exceed whatever pleasure you derive from gambling...or any sin for that matter."

[1] "Thou shalt not commit adultery..." Exodus 20:14 KJV

[2] John 8: 1-11 KJV

[3] James 1:27 KJV - "Pure religion and undefiled before God and the Father is this, To visit the fatherless and widows in their affliction..."

[4] Romans 5:12 KJV "Wherefore, as by one man sin entered into the world, and death by sin; and so death passed upon all men, for that all have sinned:"

[5] Acts 26:9-11 KJV - "9 I (Paul) verily thought with myself, that I ought to do many things contrary to the name of Jesus of Nazareth. 10 Which thing I also did in Jerusalem: and many of the saints did I shut up in prison, having received authority from the chief priests; and when they were put to death, I gave my voice against them. 11 And I punished them oft in every synagogue, and compelled them to blaspheme; and being exceedingly mad against them, I persecuted them even unto strange cities."

[6] Acts 9:3-4 KJV - "3 And as he (Paul) journeyed, he came near Damascus: and suddenly there shined round about him a light from heaven: 4 And he fell to the earth, and heard a voice saying unto him, Saul, Saul, why persecutest thou me (Jesus)?"

[7] 1 Timothy 6:10 KJV "For the love of money is the root of all evil which while some coveted after, they have erred from the faith, and pierced themselves through with many sorrows."

[8] Philippians 4:6-7 KJV "6 Be careful for nothing; but in every thing by prayer and supplication with thanksgiving let your requests be made known unto God. 7 And the peace of God, which passeth all understanding, shall keep your hearts and minds through Christ Jesus."

[9] Revelation 20:12 KJV "And I saw the dead, small and great, stand before God; and the books were opened: and another book was opened, which is the book of life: and the dead were judged out of those things which were written in the books, according to their works."

[10] 1 Corinthians 6:9-10 KJV

[11] Revelation 20:12 KJV "And I saw the dead, small and great, stand before God; and the books were opened: and another book was opened, which is the book of life: and the dead were judged out of those things which were written in the books, according to their works."

[12] Matthew 5:44 KJV